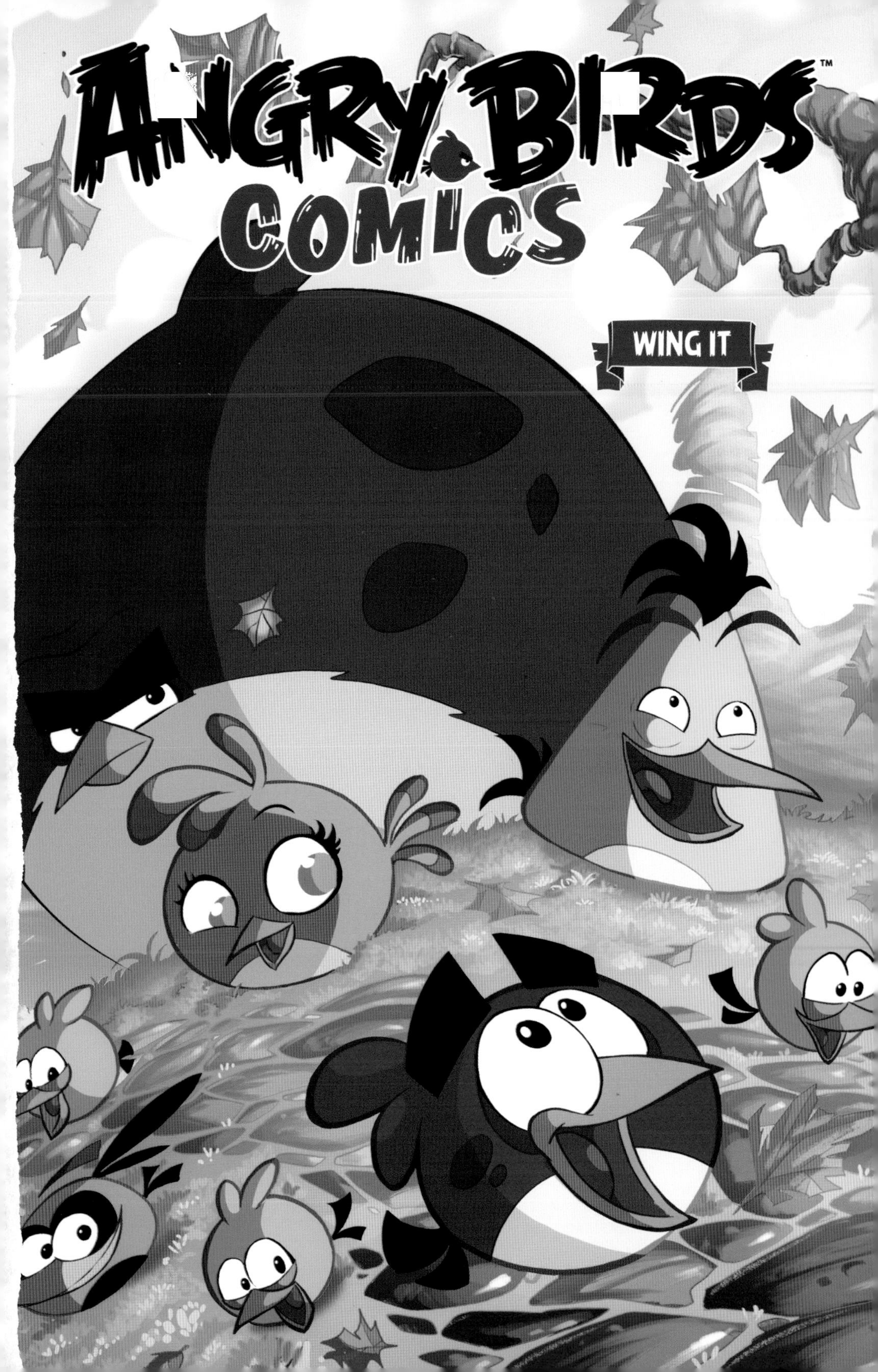
ANGRY BIRDS™
COMICS
WING IT

COVER ARTWORK BY: PACO RODRIQUES
COVER COLORS BY: NICOLA PASQUETTO

TITLE PAGE ARTWORK BY: CIRO CANGIALOSI

EDITED FOR IDW BY: DAVID HEDGECOCK
COLLECTION EDITS BY: JUSTIN EISINGER & ALONZO SIMON
COLLECTION PRODUCTION BY: CHRIS MOWRY
PUBLISHER: TED ADAMS

KAIKEN
PUBLISHING LTD.

Mikael Hed, Chairman of the Board
Laura Nevanlinna, Publishing Director
Jukka Heiskanen, Editor-in-Chief, Comics
Juha Mäkinen, Editor, Comics
Terhi Haikonen, AD
Nathan Cosby, Freelance Editor

ROVIO

Thanks to Jukka Heiskanen, Juha Mäkinen, and the Kaiken team for their hard work and invaluable assistance. For international rights, contact licensing@idwpublishing.com

ISBN: 978-1-63140-851-9

20 19 18 17   1 2 3 4

www.IDWPUBLISHING.com

Ted Adams, CEO & Publisher • Greg Goldstein, President & COO • Robbie Robbins, EVP/Sr. Graphic Artist • Chris Ryall, Chief Creative Officer •
David Hedgecock, Editor-in-Chief • Laurie Windrow, Senior Vice President of Sales & Marketing • Matthew Ruzicka, CPA, Chief Financial Officer •
Dirk Wood, VP of Marketing • Lorelei Bunjes, VP of Digital Services • Jeff Webber, VP of Licensing, Digital and Subsidiary Rights • Jerry Bennington,
VP of New Product Development

Facebook: facebook.com/idwpublishing • Twitter: @idwpublishing • YouTube: youtube.com/idwpublishing

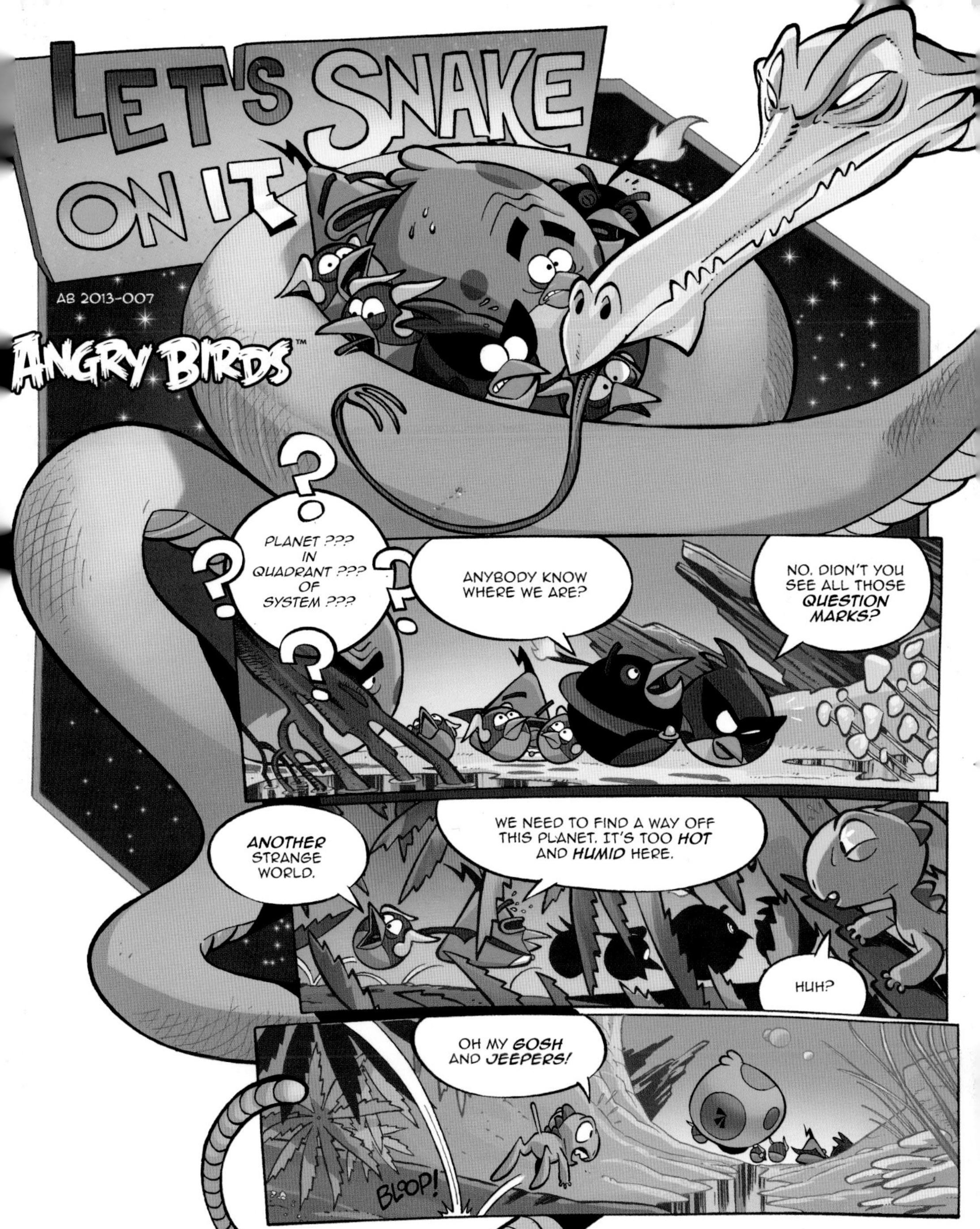
LET'S SNAKE ON IT
AB 2013-007
ANGRY BIRDS™
PLANET ??? IN QUADRANT ??? OF SYSTEM ???
ANYBODY KNOW WHERE WE ARE?
NO. DIDN'T YOU SEE ALL THOSE QUESTION MARKS?
ANOTHER STRANGE WORLD.
WE NEED TO FIND A WAY OFF THIS PLANET. IT'S TOO HOT AND HUMID HERE.
HUH?
OH MY GOSH AND JEEPERS!
BLOOP!

WRITTEN BY: PAUL TOBIN
ART BY: PACO RODRIQUES
COLORS BY: NICOLA PASQUETTO
LETTERS BY: PISARA OY

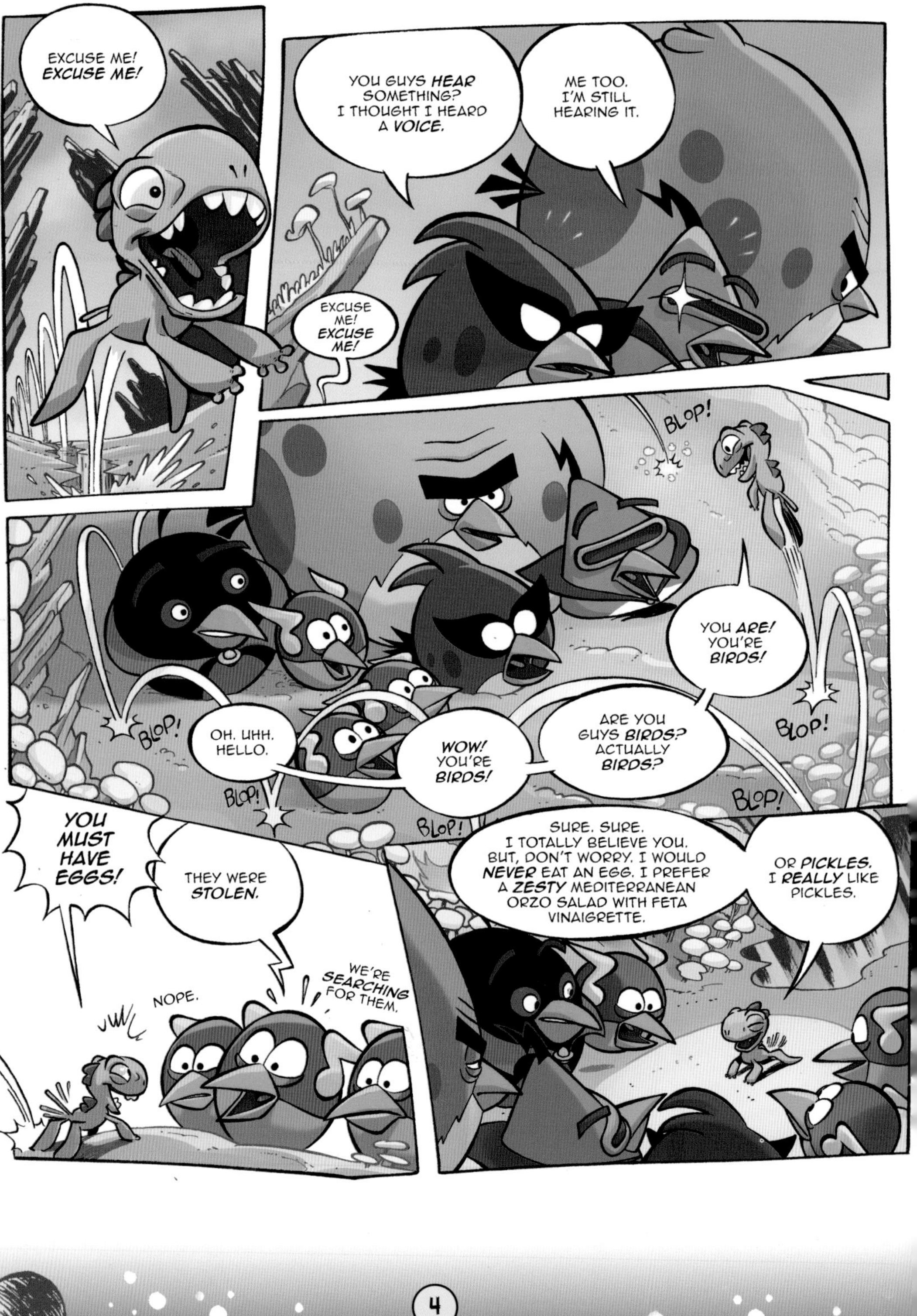
EXCUSE ME! EXCUSE ME!
YOU GUYS HEAR SOMETHING? I THOUGHT I HEARD A VOICE.
ME TOO. I'M STILL HEARING IT.
EXCUSE ME! EXCUSE ME!
BLOP!
YOU ARE! YOU'RE BIRDS!
ARE YOU GUYS BIRDS? ACTUALLY BIRDS?
WOW! YOU'RE BIRDS!
OH. UHH. HELLO.
BLOP!
BLOP!
BLOP!
BLOP!
BLOP!
YOU MUST HAVE EGGS!
THEY WERE STOLEN.
NOPE.
WE'RE SEARCHING FOR THEM.
SURE. SURE. I TOTALLY BELIEVE YOU. BUT, DON'T WORRY. I WOULD NEVER EAT AN EGG. I PREFER A ZESTY MEDITERRANEAN ORZO SALAD WITH FETA VINAIGRETTE.
OR PICKLES. I REALLY LIKE PICKLES.

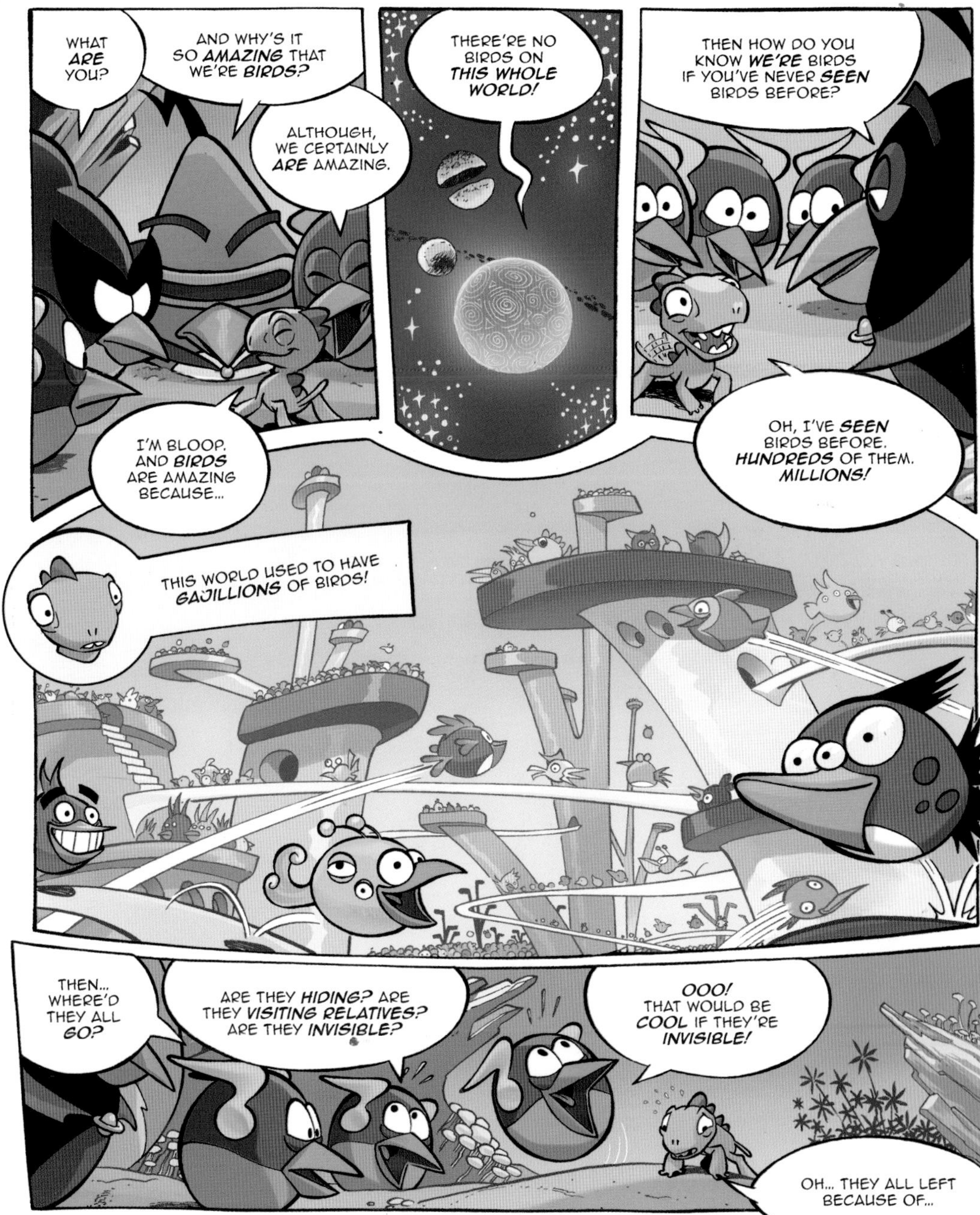
WHAT ARE YOU?
AND WHY'S IT SO AMAZING THAT WE'RE BIRDS?
ALTHOUGH, WE CERTAINLY ARE AMAZING.
THERE'RE NO BIRDS ON THIS WHOLE WORLD!
THEN HOW DO YOU KNOW WE'RE BIRDS IF YOU'VE NEVER SEEN BIRDS BEFORE?
I'M BLOOP. AND BIRDS ARE AMAZING BECAUSE...
OH, I'VE SEEN BIRDS BEFORE. HUNDREDS OF THEM. MILLIONS!
THIS WORLD USED TO HAVE GAJILLIONS OF BIRDS!
THEN... WHERE'D THEY ALL GO?
ARE THEY HIDING? ARE THEY VISITING RELATIVES? ARE THEY INVISIBLE?
OOO! THAT WOULD BE COOL IF THEY'RE INVISIBLE!
OH... THEY ALL LEFT BECAUSE OF...

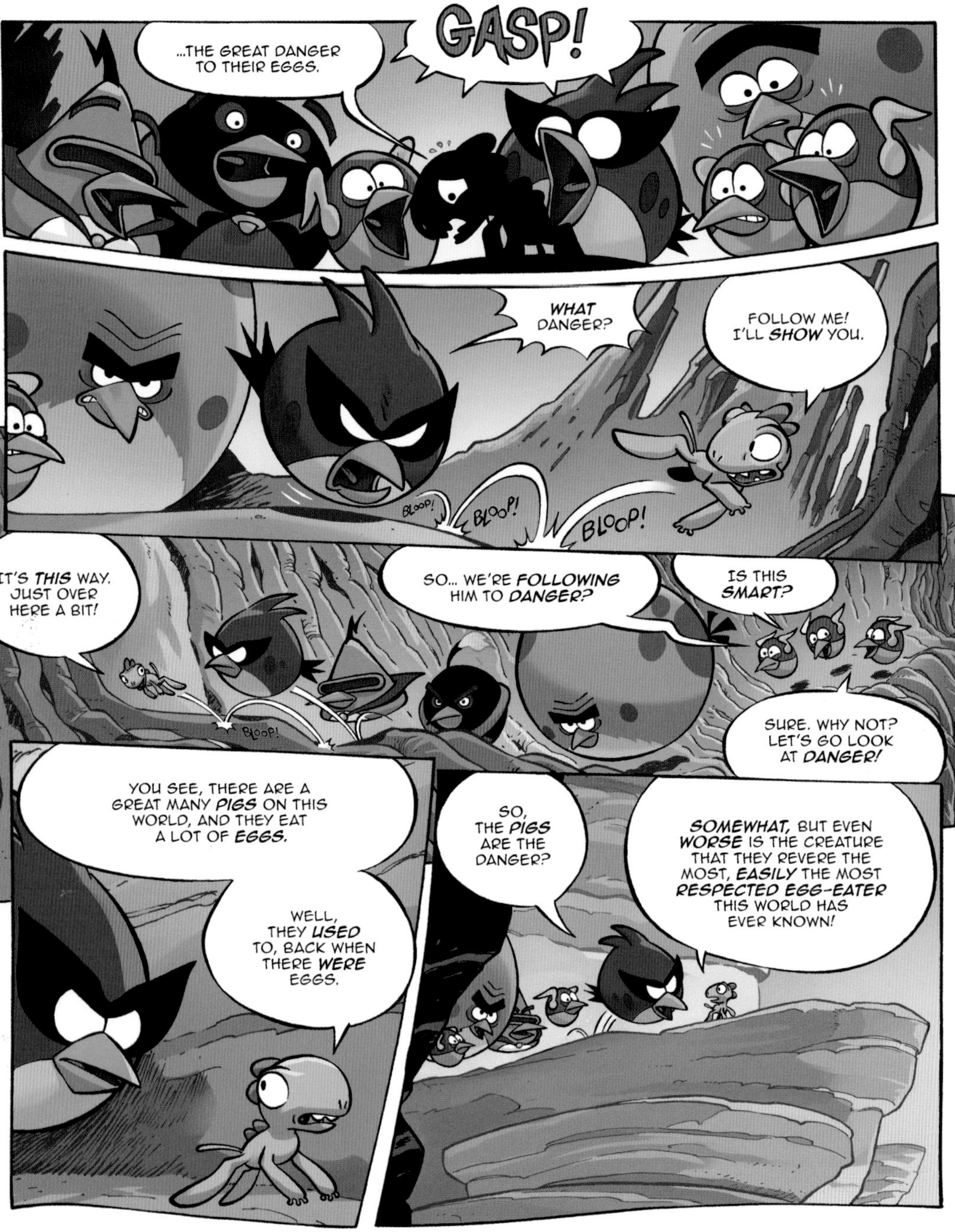
...THE GREAT DANGER TO THEIR EGGS.
GASP!
WHAT DANGER?
FOLLOW ME! I'LL SHOW YOU.
BLOOP!
BLOOP!
BLOOP!
IT'S THIS WAY. JUST OVER HERE A BIT!
SO... WE'RE FOLLOWING HIM TO DANGER?
IS THIS SMART?
BLOOP!
SURE. WHY NOT? LET'S GO LOOK AT DANGER!
YOU SEE, THERE ARE A GREAT MANY PIGS ON THIS WORLD, AND THEY EAT A LOT OF EGGS.
WELL, THEY USED TO, BACK WHEN THERE WERE EGGS.
SO, THE PIGS ARE THE DANGER?
SOMEWHAT, BUT EVEN WORSE IS THE CREATURE THAT THEY REVERE THE MOST, EASILY THE MOST RESPECTED EGG-EATER THIS WORLD HAS EVER KNOWN!

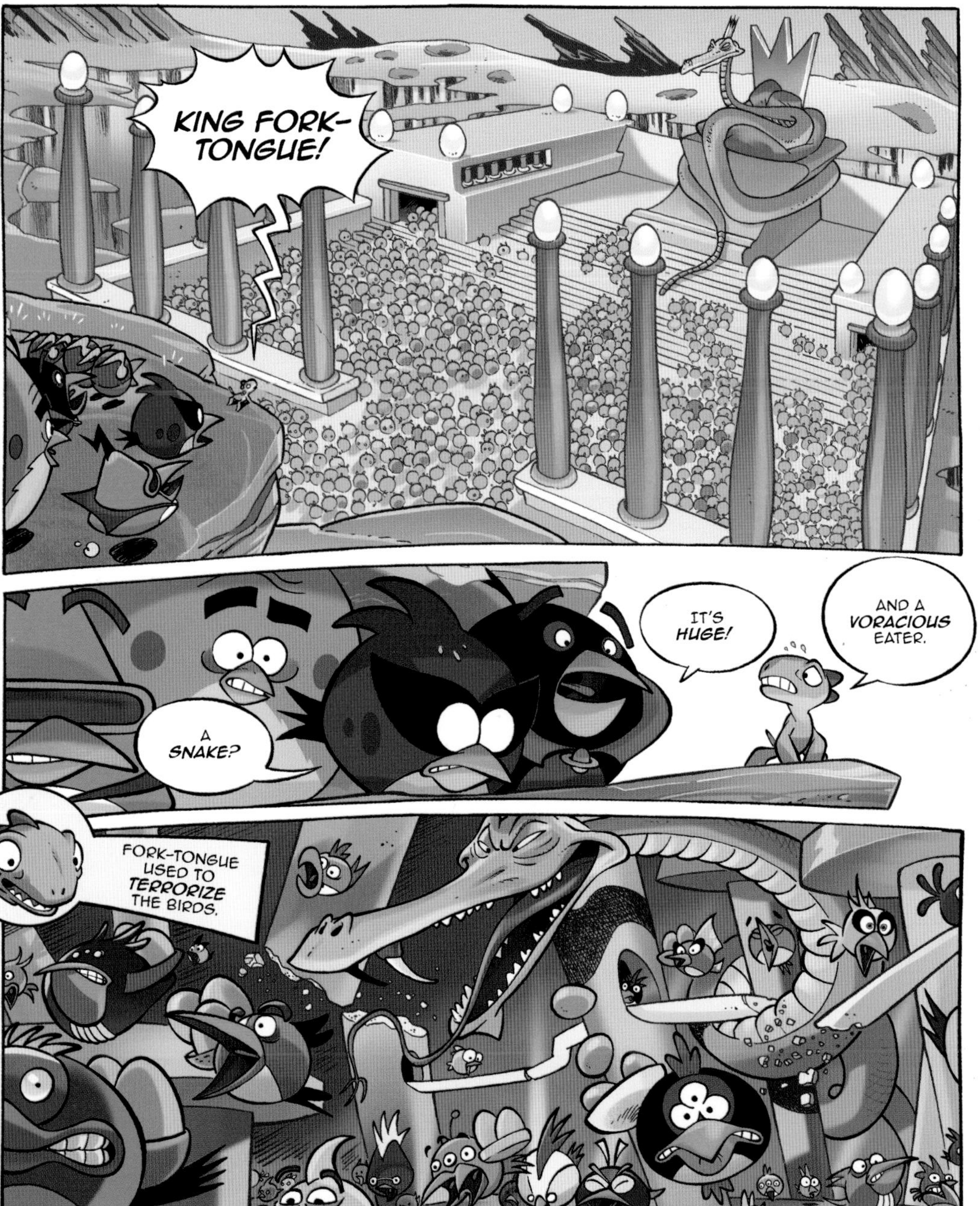
KING FORK-TONGUE!
A SNAKE?
IT'S HUGE!
AND A VORACIOUS EATER.
FORK-TONGUE USED TO TERRORIZE THE BIRDS.

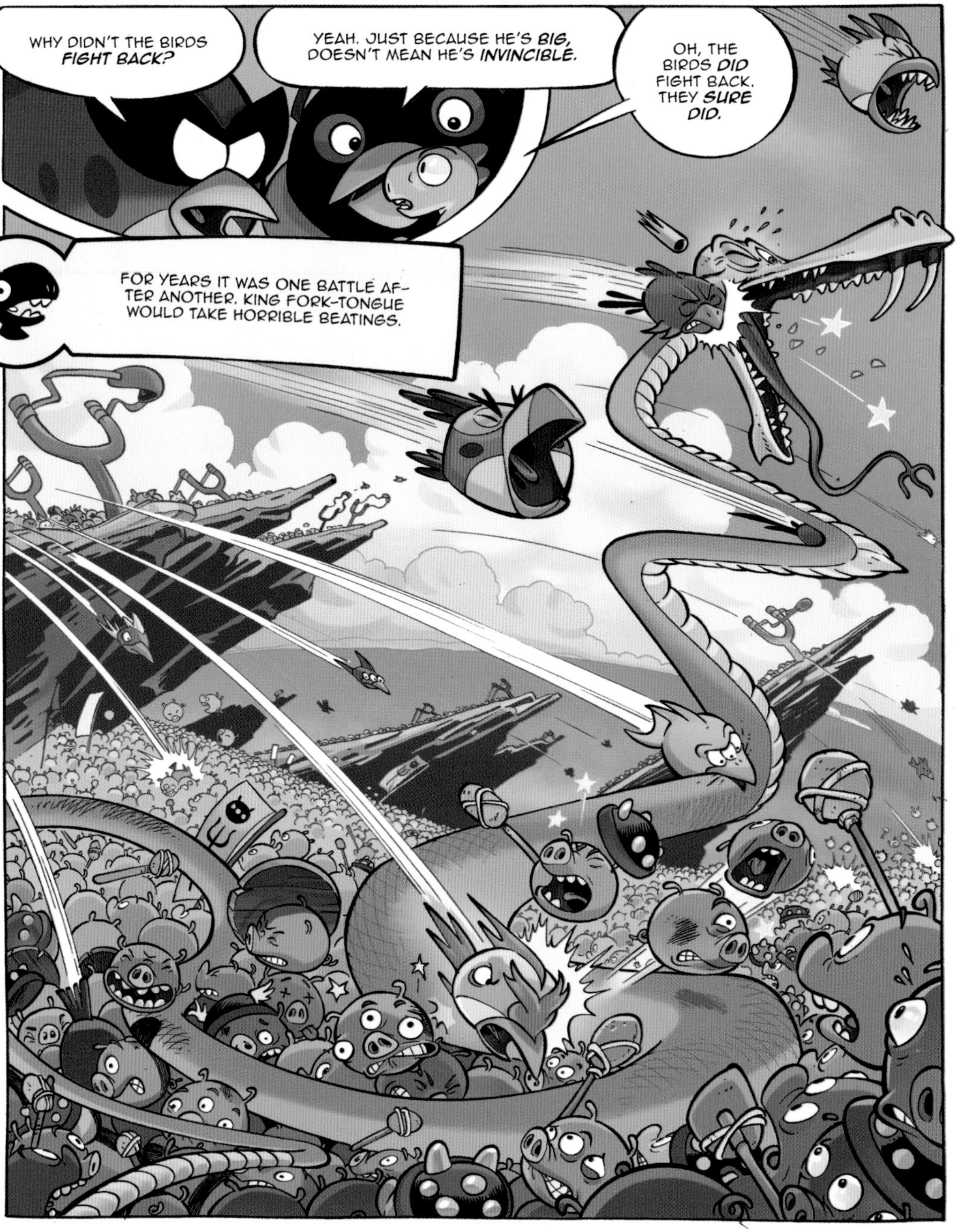
WHY DIDN'T THE BIRDS FIGHT BACK?
YEAH. JUST BECAUSE HE'S BIG, DOESN'T MEAN HE'S INVINCIBLE.
OH, THE BIRDS DID FIGHT BACK. THEY SURE DID.
FOR YEARS IT WAS ONE BATTLE AFTER ANOTHER. KING FORK-TONGUE WOULD TAKE HORRIBLE BEATINGS.

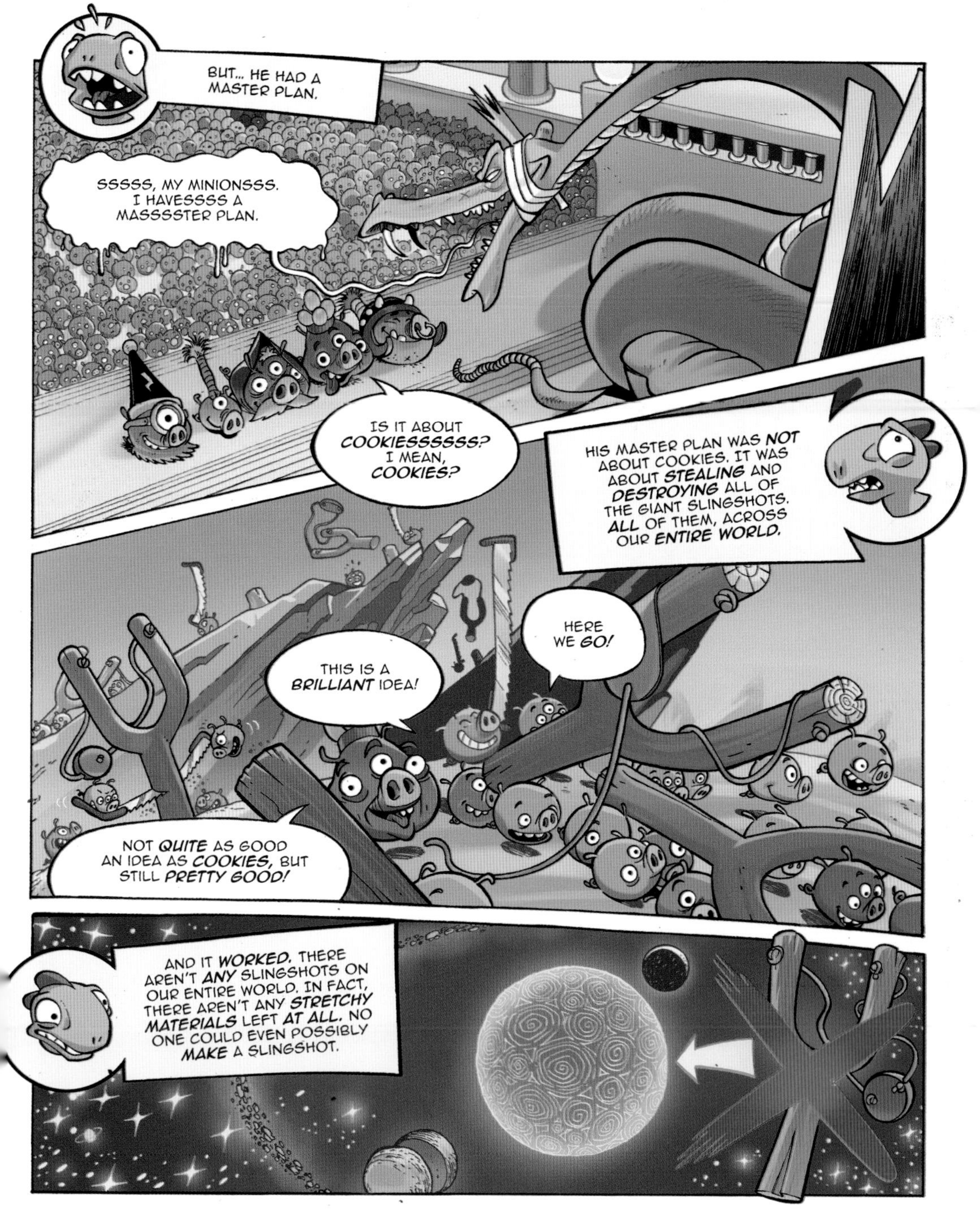
BUT... HE HAD A MASTER PLAN.
SSSSS, MY MINIONSSS. I HAVESSSS A MASSSSTER PLAN.
IS IT ABOUT COOKIESSSSSS? I MEAN, COOKIES?
HIS MASTER PLAN WAS NOT ABOUT COOKIES. IT WAS ABOUT STEALING AND DESTROYING ALL OF THE GIANT SLINGSHOTS. ALL OF THEM, ACROSS OUR ENTIRE WORLD.
THIS IS A BRILLIANT IDEA!
HERE WE GO!
NOT QUITE AS GOOD AN IDEA AS COOKIES, BUT STILL PRETTY GOOD!
AND IT WORKED. THERE AREN'T ANY SLINGSHOTS ON OUR ENTIRE WORLD. IN FACT, THERE AREN'T ANY STRETCHY MATERIALS LEFT AT ALL. NO ONE COULD EVEN POSSIBLY MAKE A SLINGSHOT.

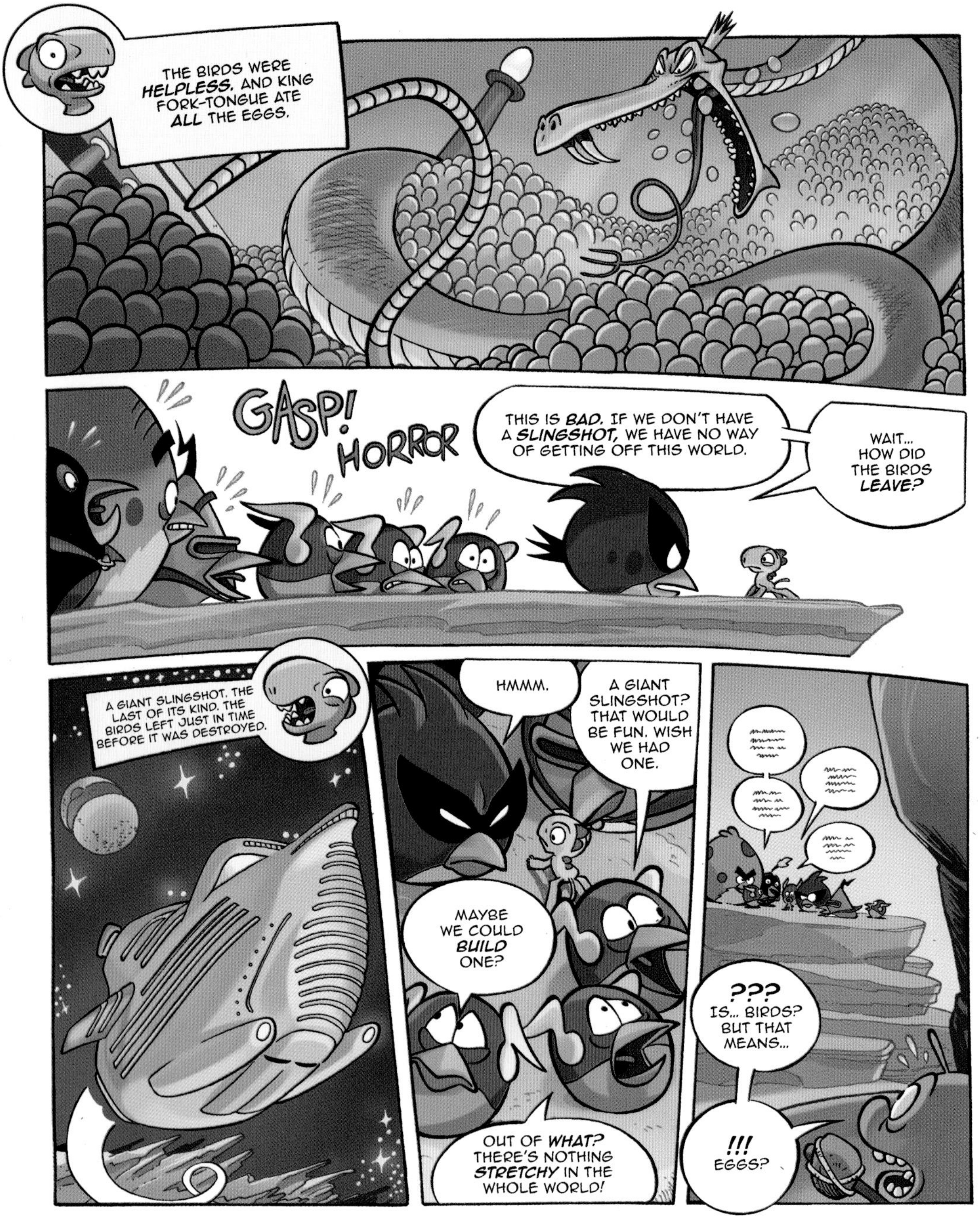
THE BIRDS WERE HELPLESS, AND KING FORK-TONGUE ATE ALL THE EGGS.
GASP!
HORROR
THIS IS BAD. IF WE DON'T HAVE A SLINGSHOT, WE HAVE NO WAY OF GETTING OFF THIS WORLD.
WAIT... HOW DID THE BIRDS LEAVE?
A GIANT SLINGSHOT. THE LAST OF ITS KIND. THE BIRDS LEFT JUST IN TIME BEFORE IT WAS DESTROYED.
HMMM.
A GIANT SLINGSHOT? THAT WOULD BE FUN. WISH WE HAD ONE.
MAYBE WE COULD BUILD ONE?
OUT OF WHAT? THERE'S NOTHING STRETCHY IN THE WHOLE WORLD!
??? IS... BIRDS? BUT THAT MEANS...
!!! EGGS?

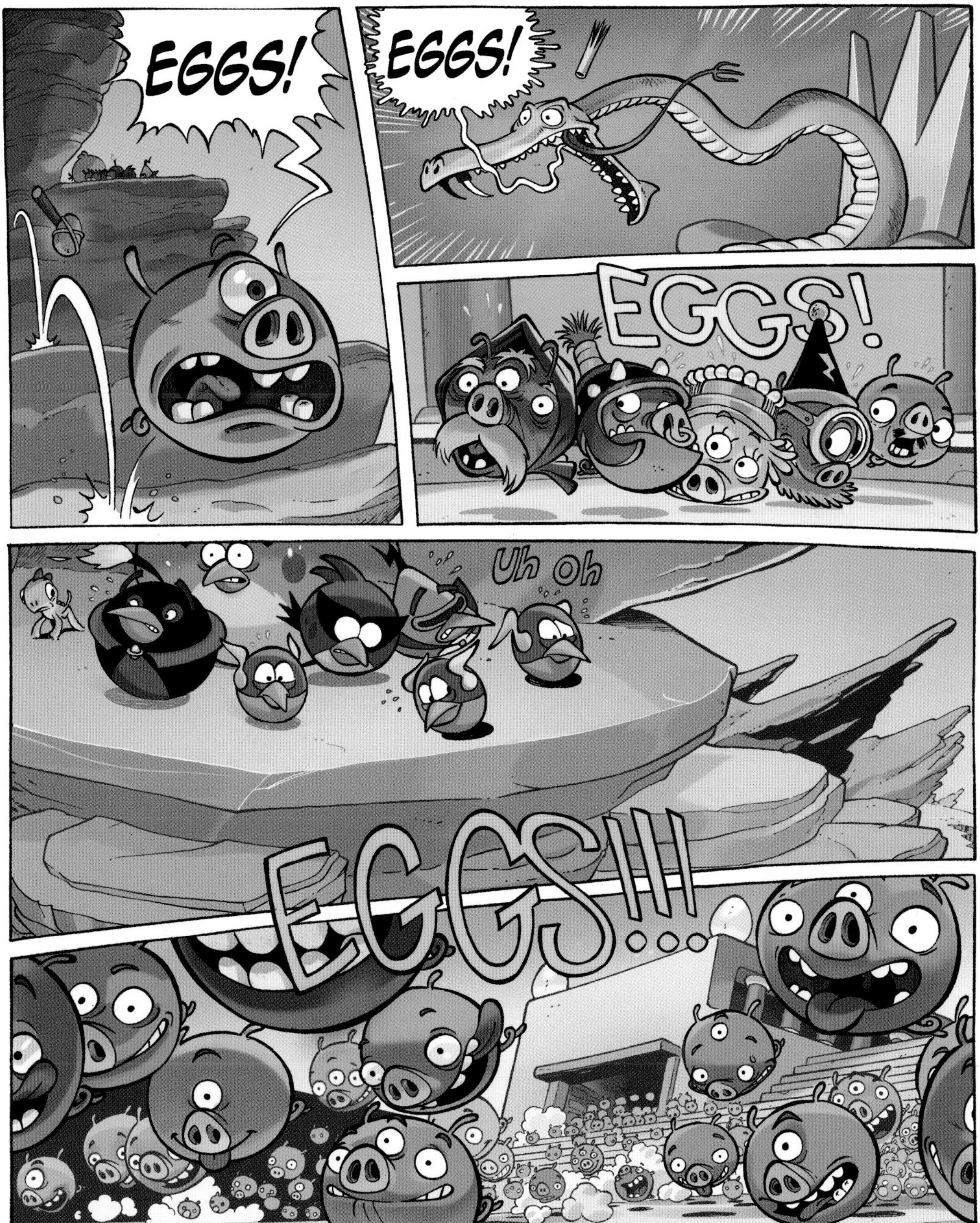
EGGS!
EGGS!
EGGS!
Uh oh
EGGS!!!

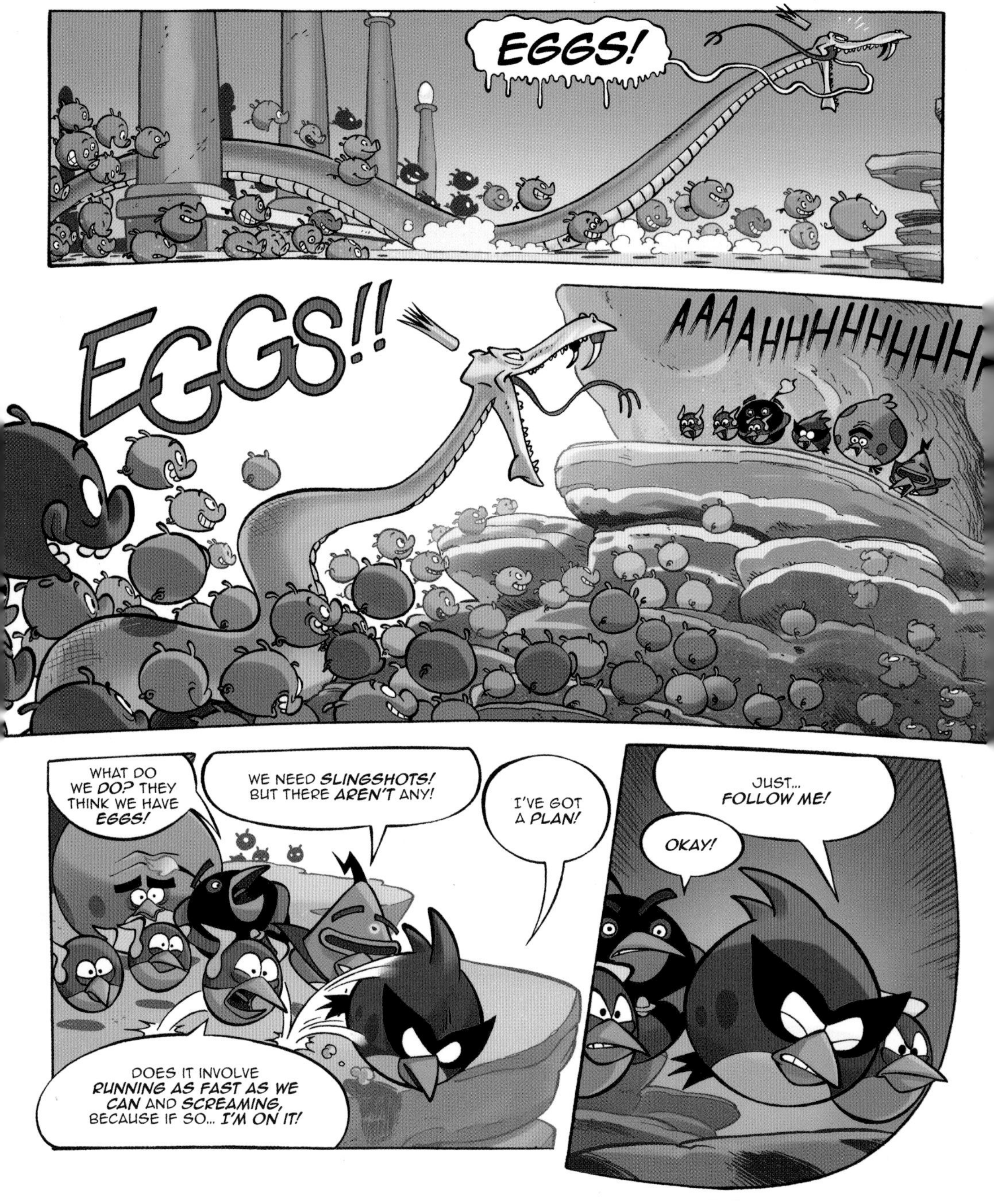
EGGS!
EGGS!!
AAAAHHHHHHHHH
WHAT DO WE DO? THEY THINK WE HAVE EGGS!
WE NEED SLINGSHOTS! BUT THERE AREN'T ANY!
I'VE GOT A PLAN!
DOES IT INVOLVE RUNNING AS FAST AS WE CAN AND SCREAMING, BECAUSE IF SO... I'M ON IT!
JUST... FOLLOW ME!
OKAY!

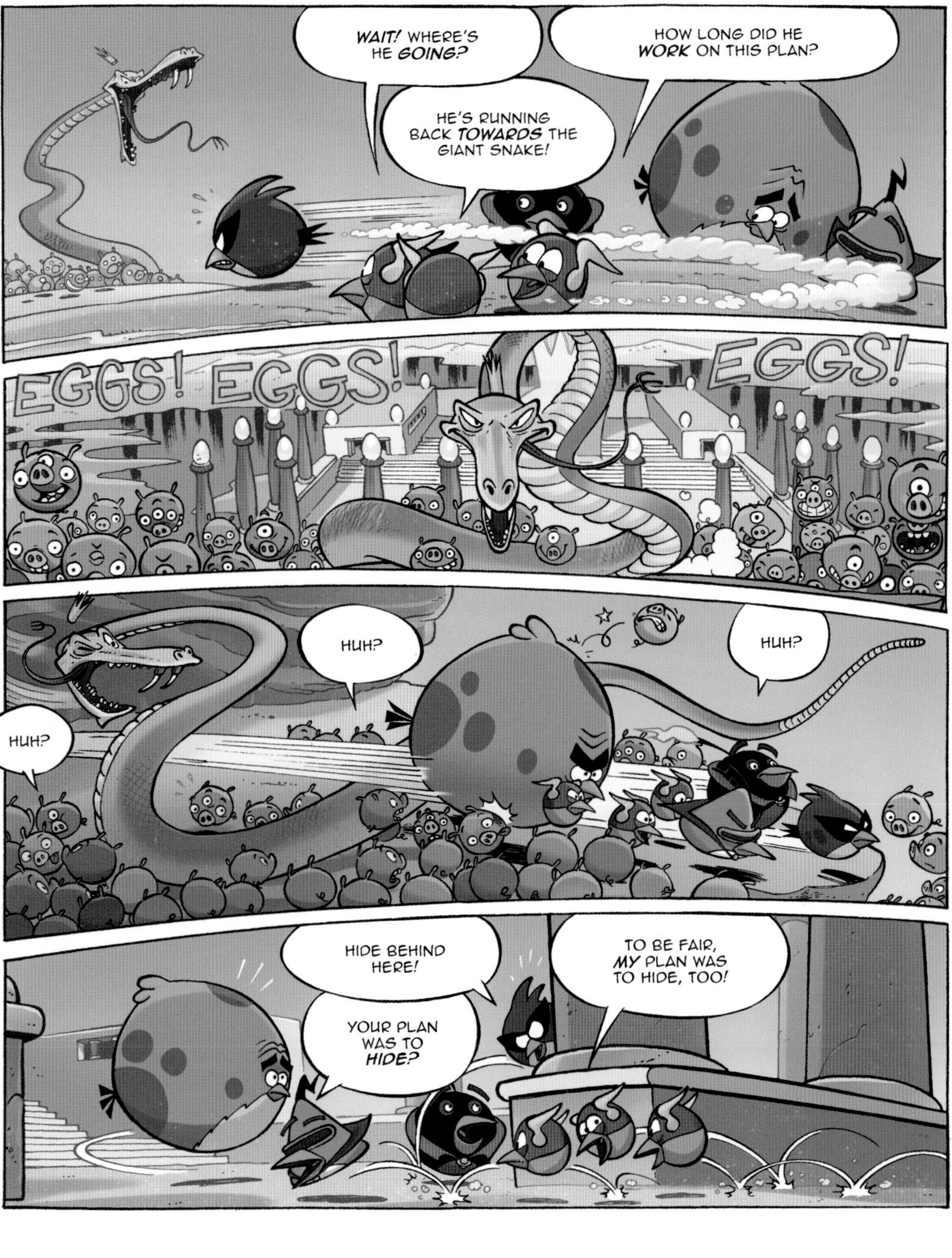
WAIT! WHERE'S HE GOING?
HE'S RUNNING BACK TOWARDS THE GIANT SNAKE!
HOW LONG DID HE WORK ON THIS PLAN?
EGGS! EGGS! EGGS!
HUH?
HUH?
HUH?
HIDE BEHIND HERE!
YOUR PLAN WAS TO HIDE?
TO BE FAIR, MY PLAN WAS TO HIDE, TOO!

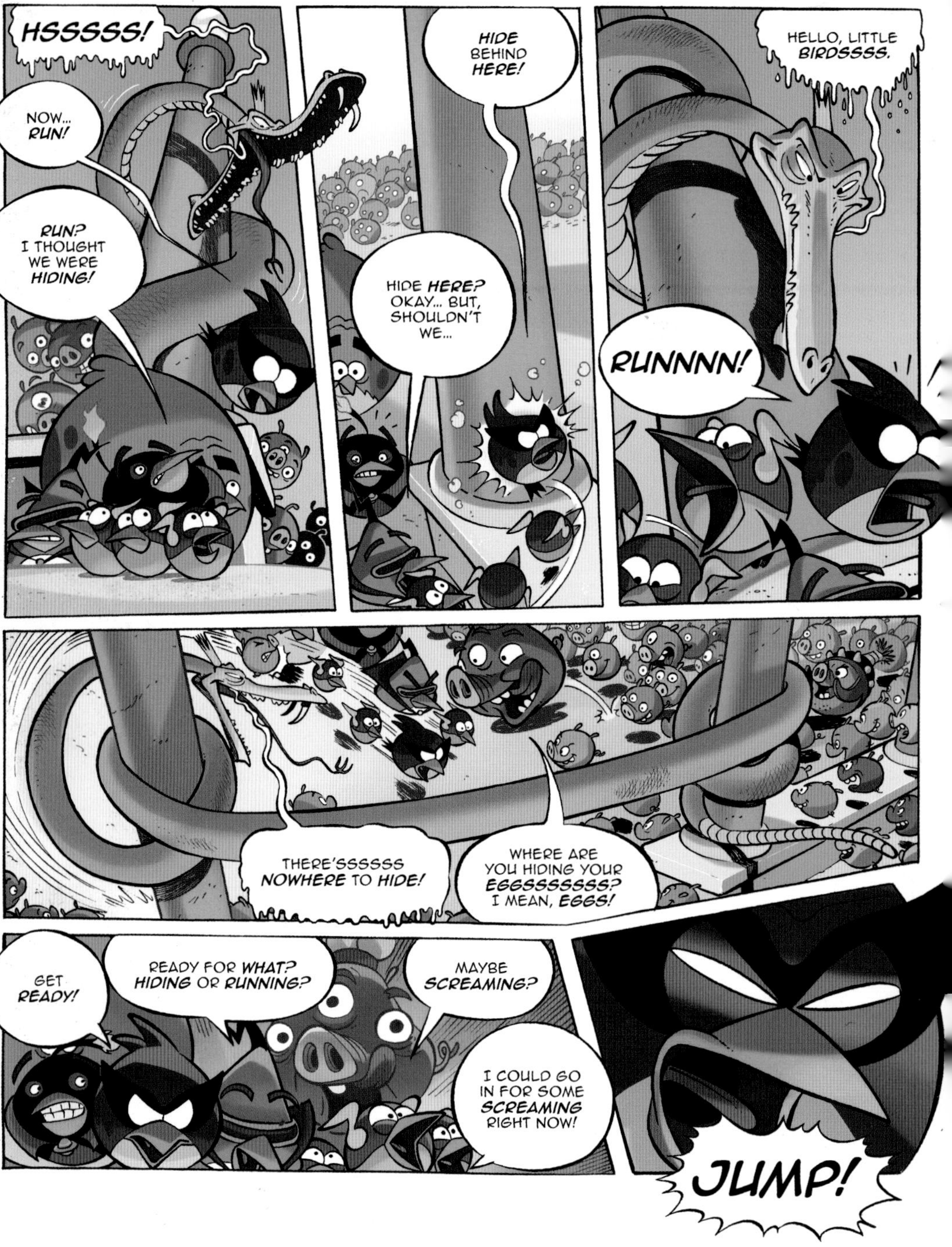
HSSSSS!
NOW... RUN!
RUN? I THOUGHT WE WERE HIDING!
HIDE BEHIND HERE!
HIDE HERE? OKAY... BUT, SHOULDN'T WE...
HELLO, LITTLE BIRDSSSS.
RUNNNN!
THERE'SSSSSS NOWHERE TO HIDE!
WHERE ARE YOU HIDING YOUR EGGSSSSSSSS? I MEAN, EGGS!
GET READY!
READY FOR WHAT? HIDING OR RUNNING?
MAYBE SCREAMING?
I COULD GO IN FOR SOME SCREAMING RIGHT NOW!
JUMP!

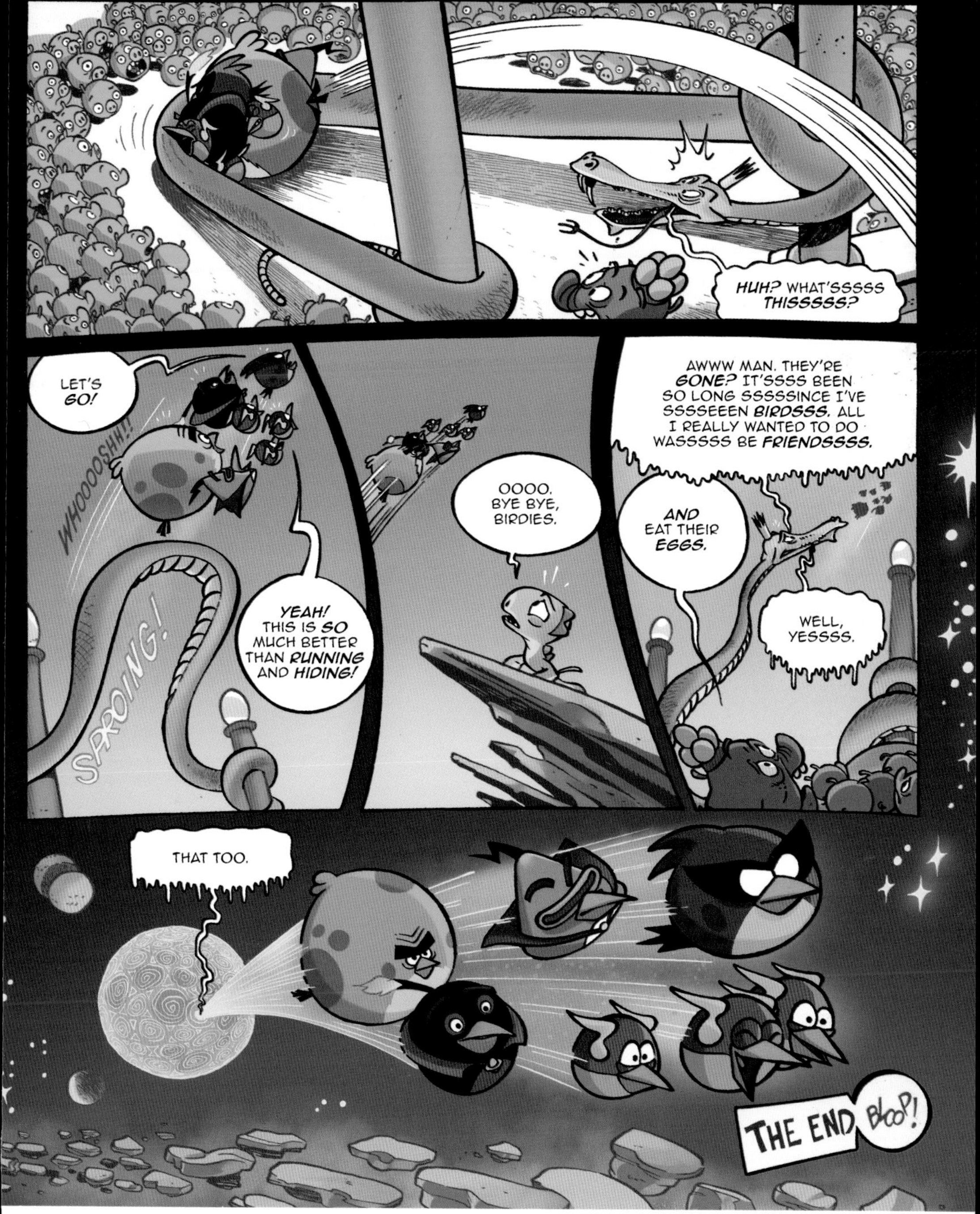
HUH? WHAT'SSSSS THISSSSS?
LET'S GO!
WHOOOOSHH!!
YEAH! THIS IS SO MUCH BETTER THAN RUNNING AND HIDING!
SPROING!
OOOO. BYE BYE, BIRDIES.
AWWW MAN. THEY'RE GONE? IT'SSSS BEEN SO LONG SSSSSINCE I'VE SSSSEEEN BIRDSSS. ALL I REALLY WANTED TO DO WASSSSS BE FRIENDSSSS.
AND EAT THEIR EGGS.
WELL, YESSSS.
THAT TOO.
THE END
BLOOP!

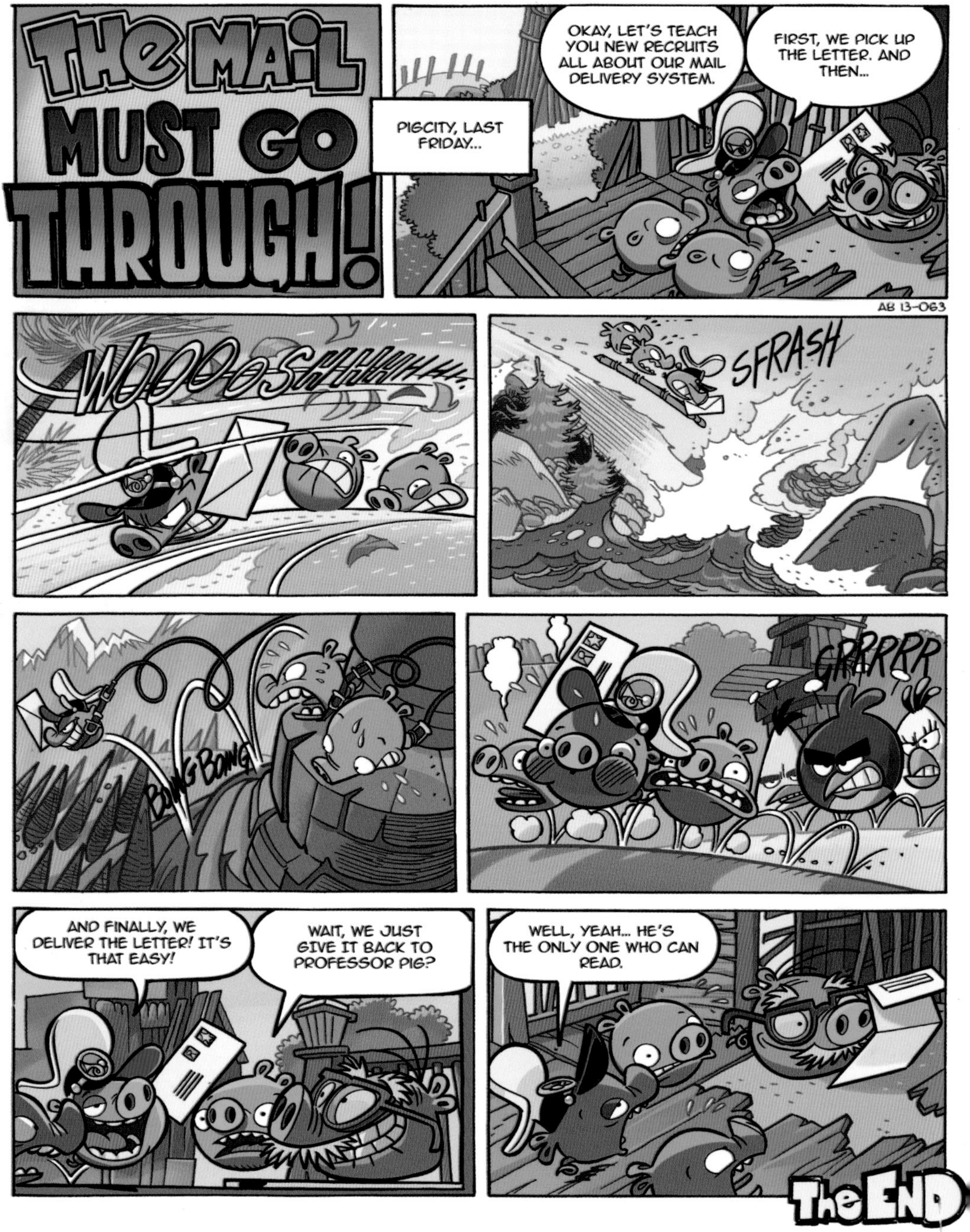
THE MAIL MUST GO THROUGH!
PIGCITY, LAST FRIDAY...
OKAY, LET'S TEACH YOU NEW RECRUITS ALL ABOUT OUR MAIL DELIVERY SYSTEM.
FIRST, WE PICK UP THE LETTER. AND THEN...
AB 13-063
WOOOOOSHHHHHH
SFRASH
BOING BOING
GRRRRR
AND FINALLY, WE DELIVER THE LETTER! IT'S THAT EASY!
WAIT, WE JUST GIVE IT BACK TO PROFESSOR PIG?
WELL, YEAH... HE'S THE ONLY ONE WHO CAN READ.
The END

WRITTEN BY: PAUL TOBIN • ART BY: CORRADO MASTANTUONO • COLORS BY: NICOLA PASQUETTO • LETTERS BY: PISARA OY

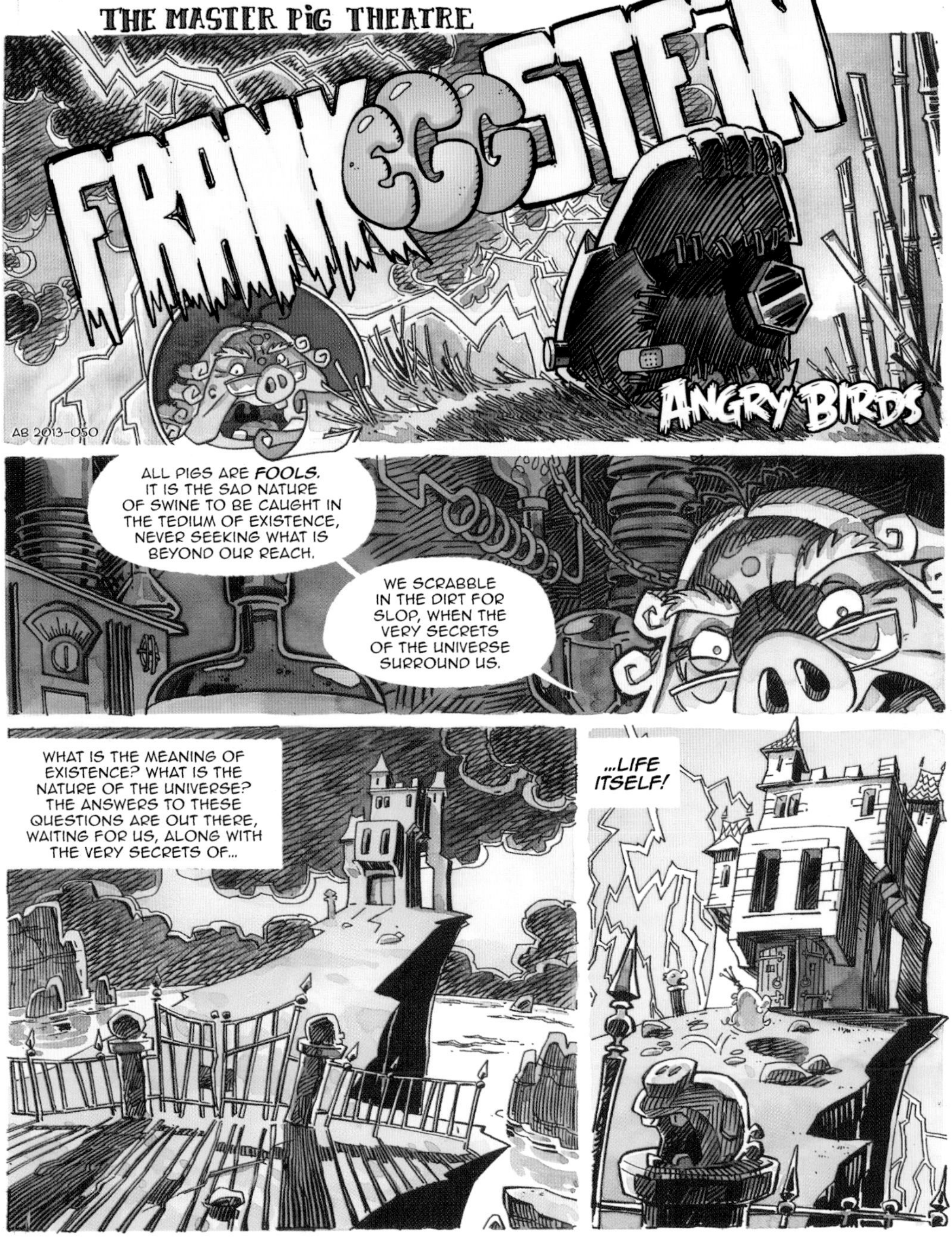
THE MASTER PIG THEATRE
FRANKEGGSTEIN
ANGRY BIRDS
AB 2013-050
ALL PIGS ARE *FOOLS.* IT IS THE SAD NATURE OF SWINE TO BE CAUGHT IN THE TEDIUM OF EXISTENCE, NEVER SEEKING WHAT IS BEYOND OUR REACH.
WE SCRABBLE IN THE DIRT FOR SLOP, WHEN THE VERY SECRETS OF THE UNIVERSE SURROUND US.
WHAT IS THE MEANING OF EXISTENCE? WHAT IS THE NATURE OF THE UNIVERSE? THE ANSWERS TO THESE QUESTIONS ARE OUT THERE, WAITING FOR US, ALONG WITH THE VERY SECRETS OF...
...LIFE ITSELF!

WRITTEN BY: PAUL TOBIN • ART & COLORS BY: JM BOESCH • LETTERS BY: PISARA OY

INSIDE, A DARKENED LABORATORY, WHERE A STRANGE QUEST BEGINS! IT IS THE CHASE FOR THE *UNKNOWN!* A VERITABLE *MADMAN'S* PURSUIT OF HIS *GREATEST DESIRE!*

I WANT AN *EGG.* MAKE ME ONE.

BUT... IS HE *TRULY* MAD? FOR, WHAT *IS* MADNESS? SHOULD WE CONSIDER IT *SANITY* TO CONFINE YOURSELF TO THE LIFE YOU ALREADY KNOW? IS IT *FOLLY* TO QUEST FOR THE UNKNOWN? IS IT *SANE* TO REMAIN *IGNORANT* IN THE FACE OF *UNIVERSAL MYSTERIES?*

HMMM. CREATE AN EGG? I'LL SEE WHAT I CAN DO.

MAYBE SOME LOLLIPOPS TOO!

AND SO, THE QUEST FOR KNOWLEDGE *BEGINS!*

MINION, BRING ME THAT *BOOK.*

WHAT'S A *"BOOK?"*

THE THING WITH *PAGES* IN IT!

WHAT'S A *"PAGE?"*

AND IT KEEPS BEGINNING...

A *PAGE* IS A SHEET OF PAPER WITH SENTENCES THAT...

WHAT ARE *"SEN-TENCES?"*

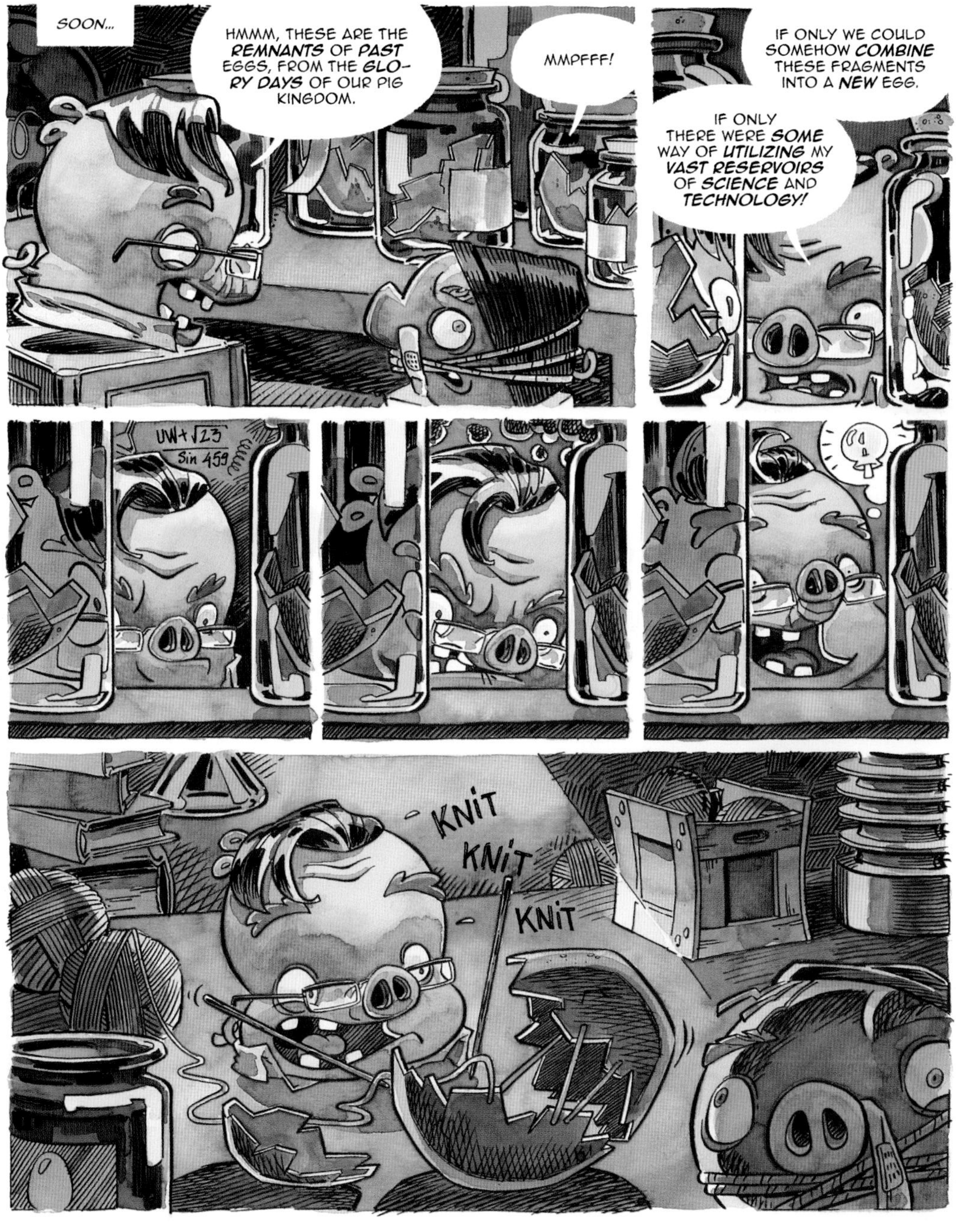
SOON...
HMMM, THESE ARE THE **REMNANTS** OF **PAST** EGGS, FROM THE **GLORY DAYS** OF OUR PIG KINGDOM.
MMPFFF!
IF ONLY WE COULD SOMEHOW **COMBINE** THESE FRAGMENTS INTO A **NEW** EGG.
IF ONLY THERE WERE **SOME** WAY OF **UTILIZING** MY **VAST RESERVOIRS** OF **SCIENCE** AND **TECHNOLOGY!**
UW + √23
Sin 459
KNIT
KNIT
KNIT

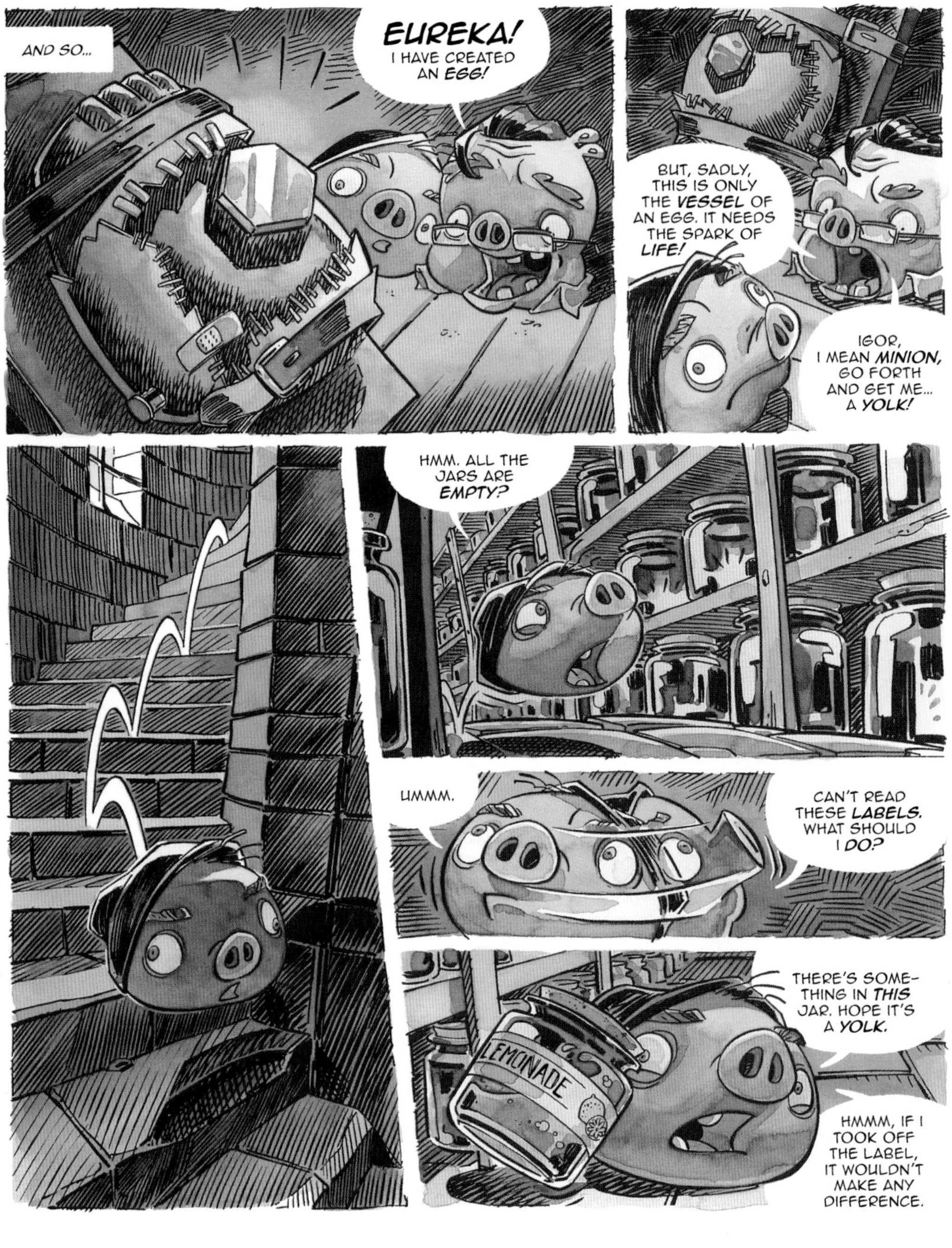

AND SO...
EUREKA! I HAVE CREATED AN EGG!
BUT, SADLY, THIS IS ONLY THE VESSEL OF AN EGG. IT NEEDS THE SPARK OF LIFE!
IGOR, I MEAN MINION, GO FORTH AND GET ME... A YOLK!
HMM. ALL THE JARS ARE EMPTY?
UMMM.
CAN'T READ THESE LABELS. WHAT SHOULD I DO?
THERE'S SOME-THING IN THIS JAR. HOPE IT'S A YOLK.
LEMONADE
HMMM, IF I TOOK OFF THE LABEL, IT WOULDN'T MAKE ANY DIFFERENCE.

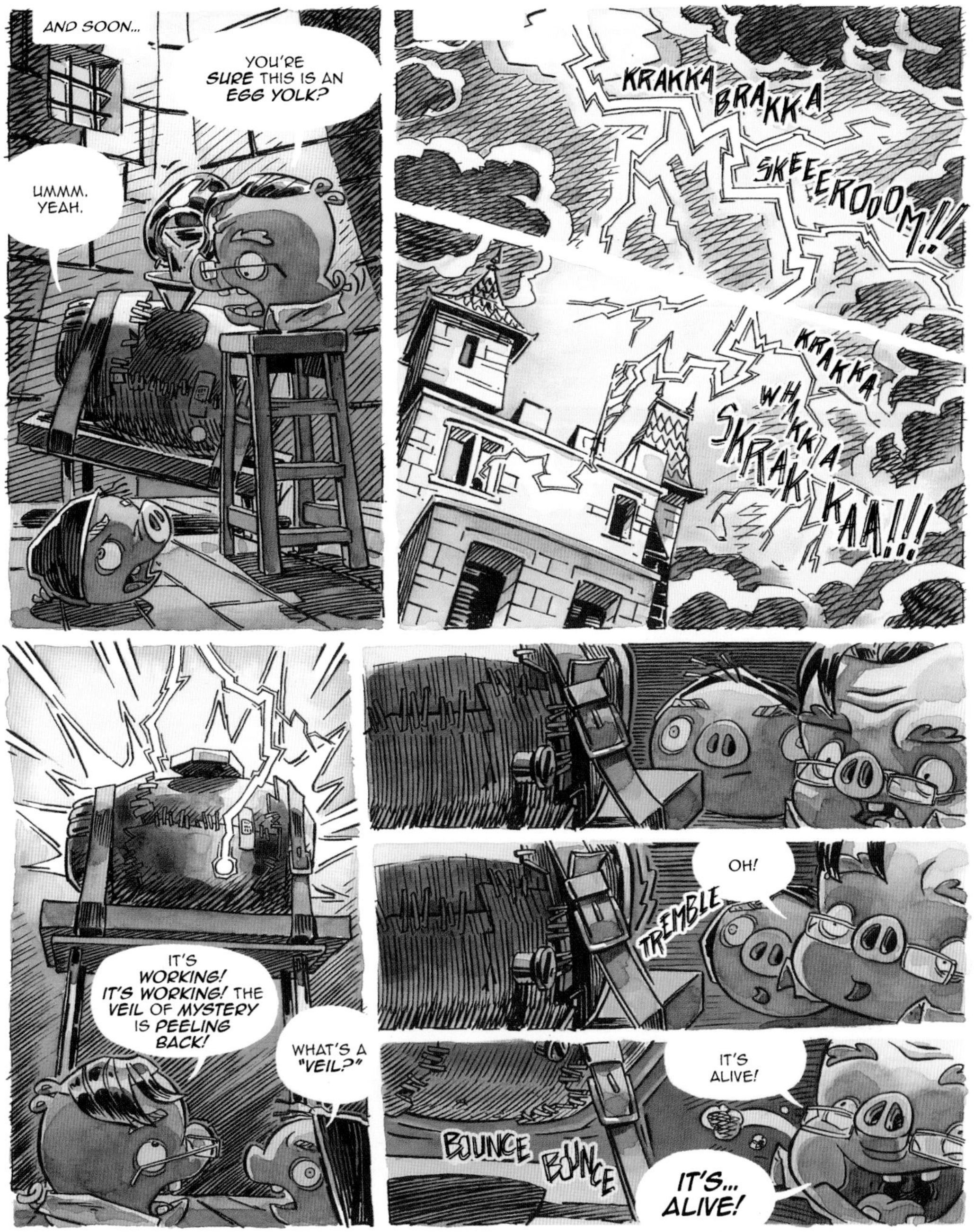
AND SOON...
YOU'RE SURE THIS IS AN EGG YOLK?
UMMM. YEAH.
KRAKKA BRAKKA
SKEEEROOOM!!
KRAKKA WHAKKA SKRAKKAA!!!
IT'S WORKING! IT'S WORKING! THE VEIL OF MYSTERY IS PEELING BACK!
WHAT'S A "VEIL?"
OH!
TREMBLE
IT'S ALIVE!
BOUNCE BOUNCE
IT'S... ALIVE!

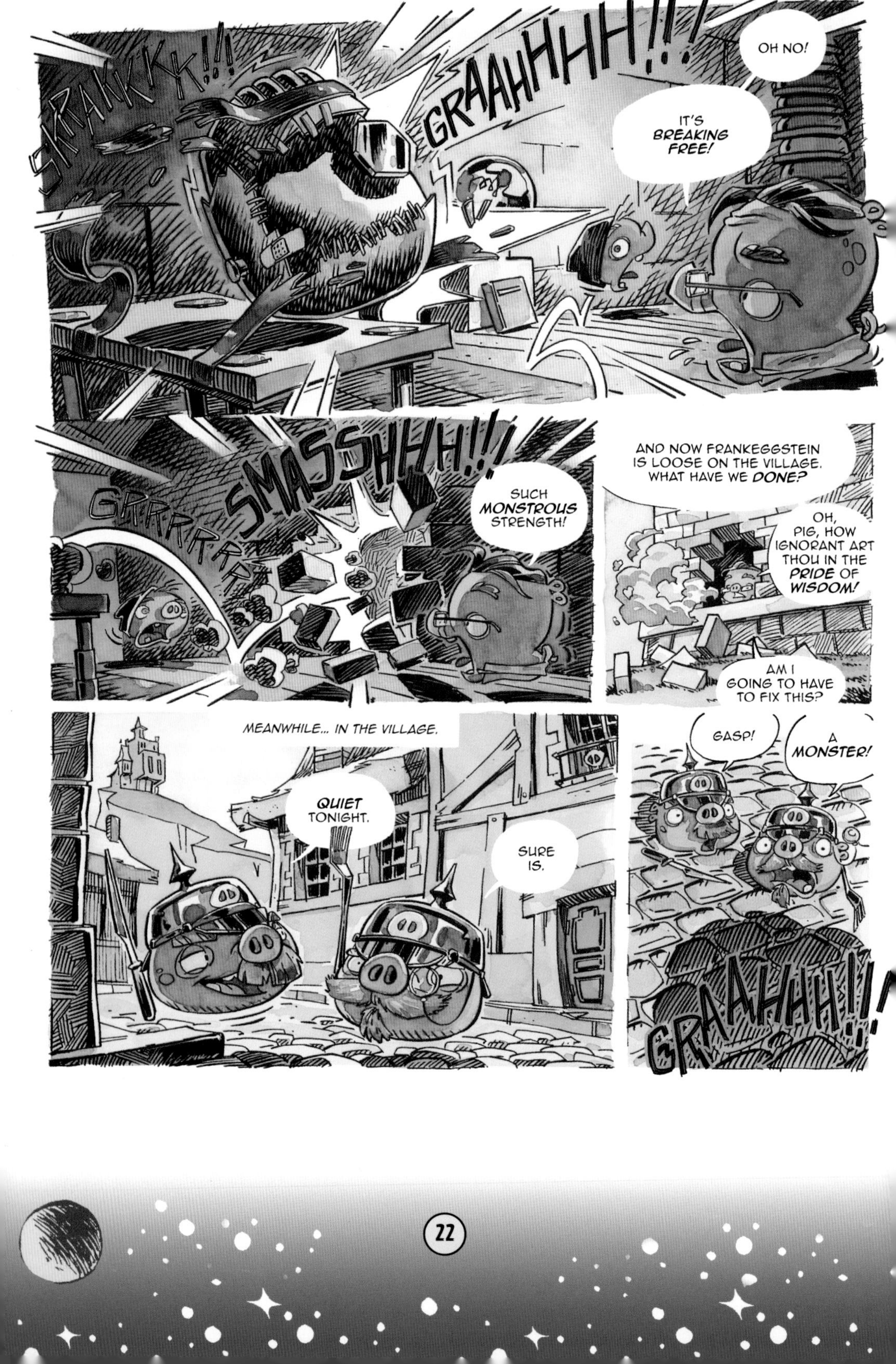

SKRAKKKK!!!
GRAAHHHH!!!
OH NO!
IT'S BREAKING FREE!
SMASSHHH!!!
GRRRRRRR
SUCH MONSTROUS STRENGTH!
AND NOW FRANKEGGSTEIN IS LOOSE ON THE VILLAGE. WHAT HAVE WE DONE?
OH, PIG, HOW IGNORANT ART THOU IN THE PRIDE OF WISDOM!
AM I GOING TO HAVE TO FIX THIS?
MEANWHILE... IN THE VILLAGE.
QUIET TONIGHT.
SURE IS.
GASP!
A MONSTER!
GRAAHHH!!!

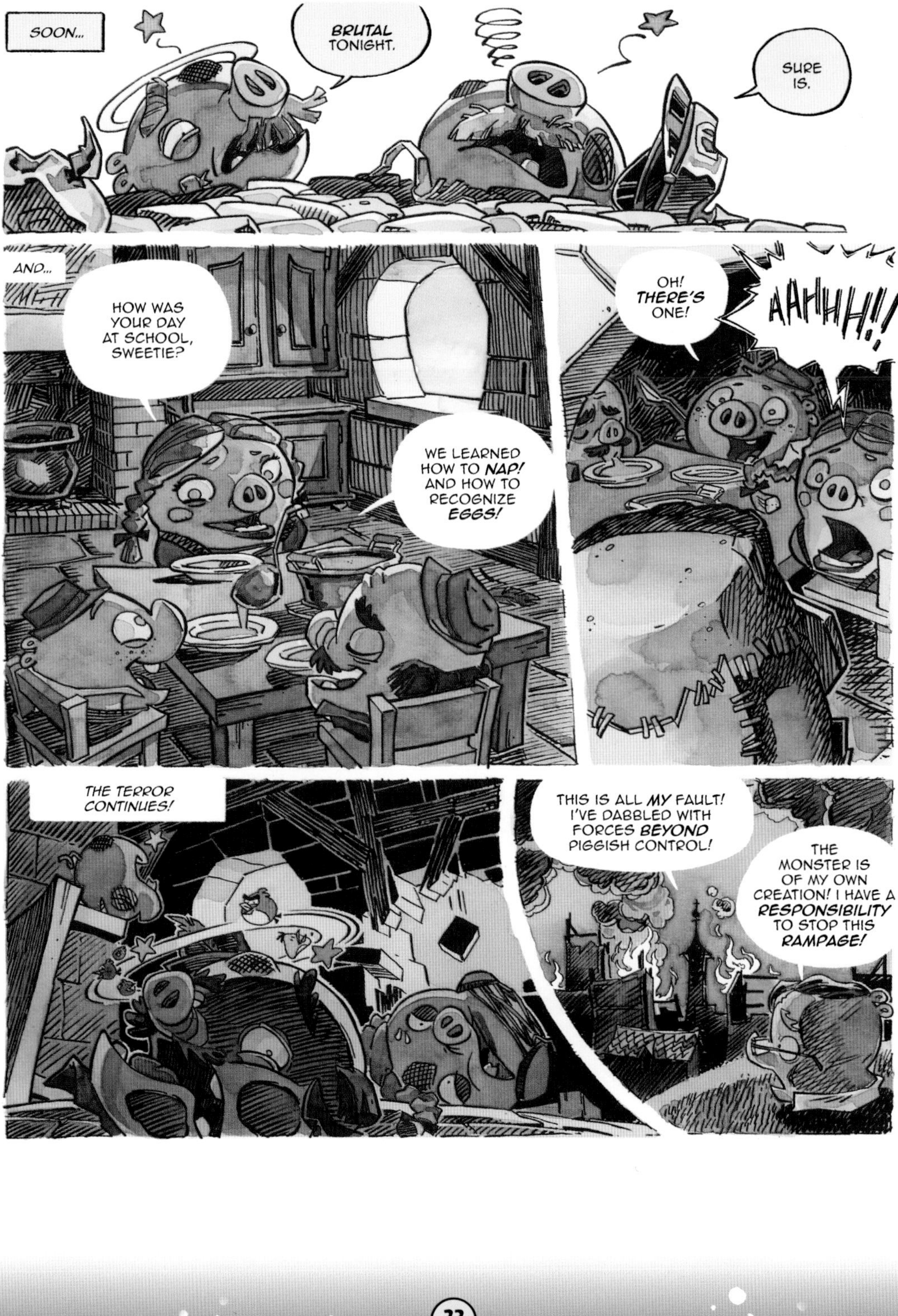
SOON...
BRUTAL TONIGHT.
SURE IS.
AND...
HOW WAS YOUR DAY AT SCHOOL, SWEETIE?
WE LEARNED HOW TO NAP! AND HOW TO RECOGNIZE EGGS!
OH! THERE'S ONE!
AHHHH!!
THE TERROR CONTINUES!
THIS IS ALL MY FAULT! I'VE DABBLED WITH FORCES BEYOND PIGGISH CONTROL!
THE MONSTER IS OF MY OWN CREATION! I HAVE A RESPONSIBILITY TO STOP THIS RAMPAGE!

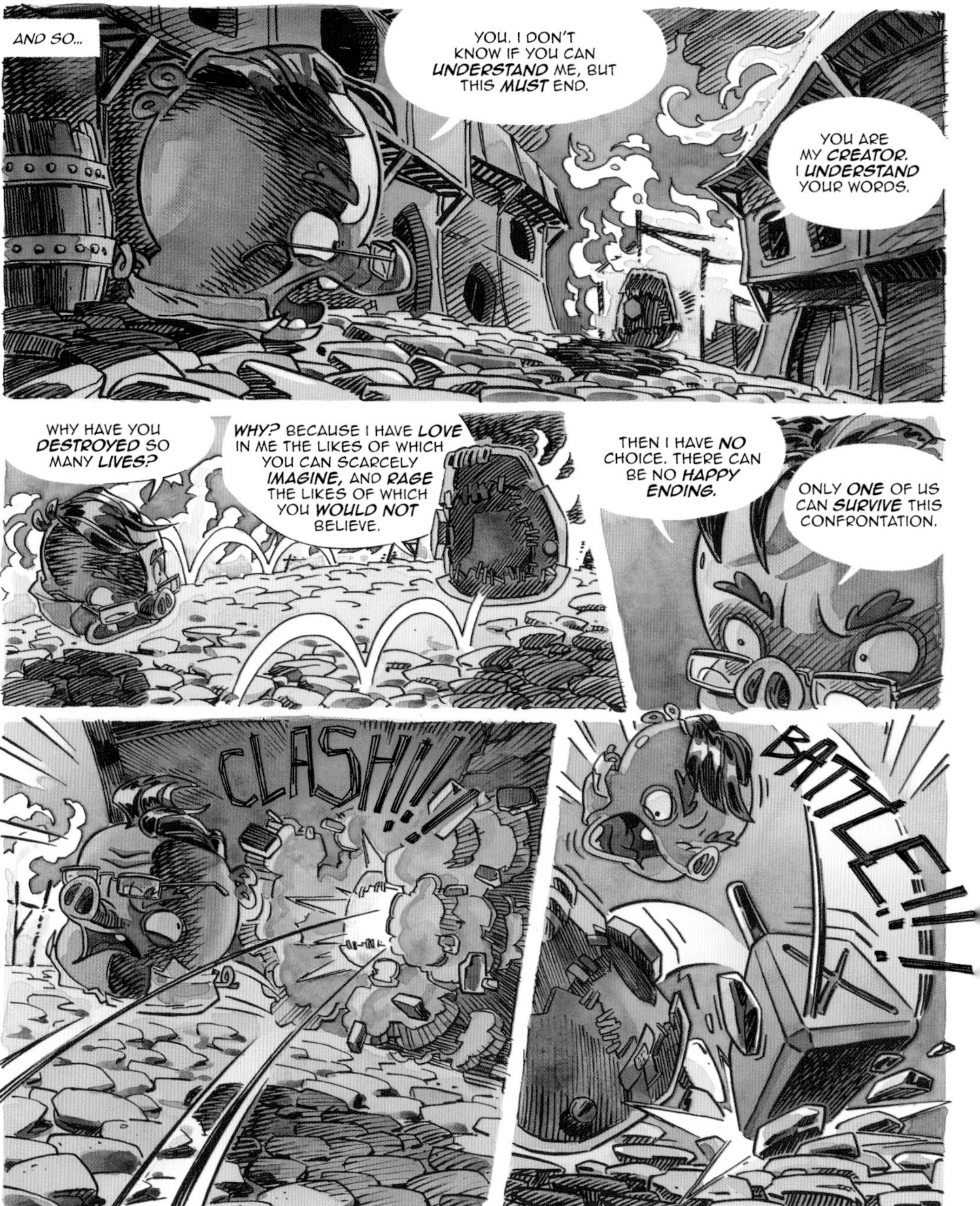
AND SO...
YOU. I DON'T KNOW IF YOU CAN UNDERSTAND ME, BUT THIS MUST END.
YOU ARE MY CREATOR. I UNDERSTAND YOUR WORDS.
WHY HAVE YOU DESTROYED SO MANY LIVES?
WHY? BECAUSE I HAVE LOVE IN ME THE LIKES OF WHICH YOU CAN SCARCELY IMAGINE, AND RAGE THE LIKES OF WHICH YOU WOULD NOT BELIEVE.
THEN I HAVE NO CHOICE. THERE CAN BE NO HAPPY ENDING.
ONLY ONE OF US CAN SURVIVE THIS CONFRONTATION.
CLASH!!!
BATTLE!!!

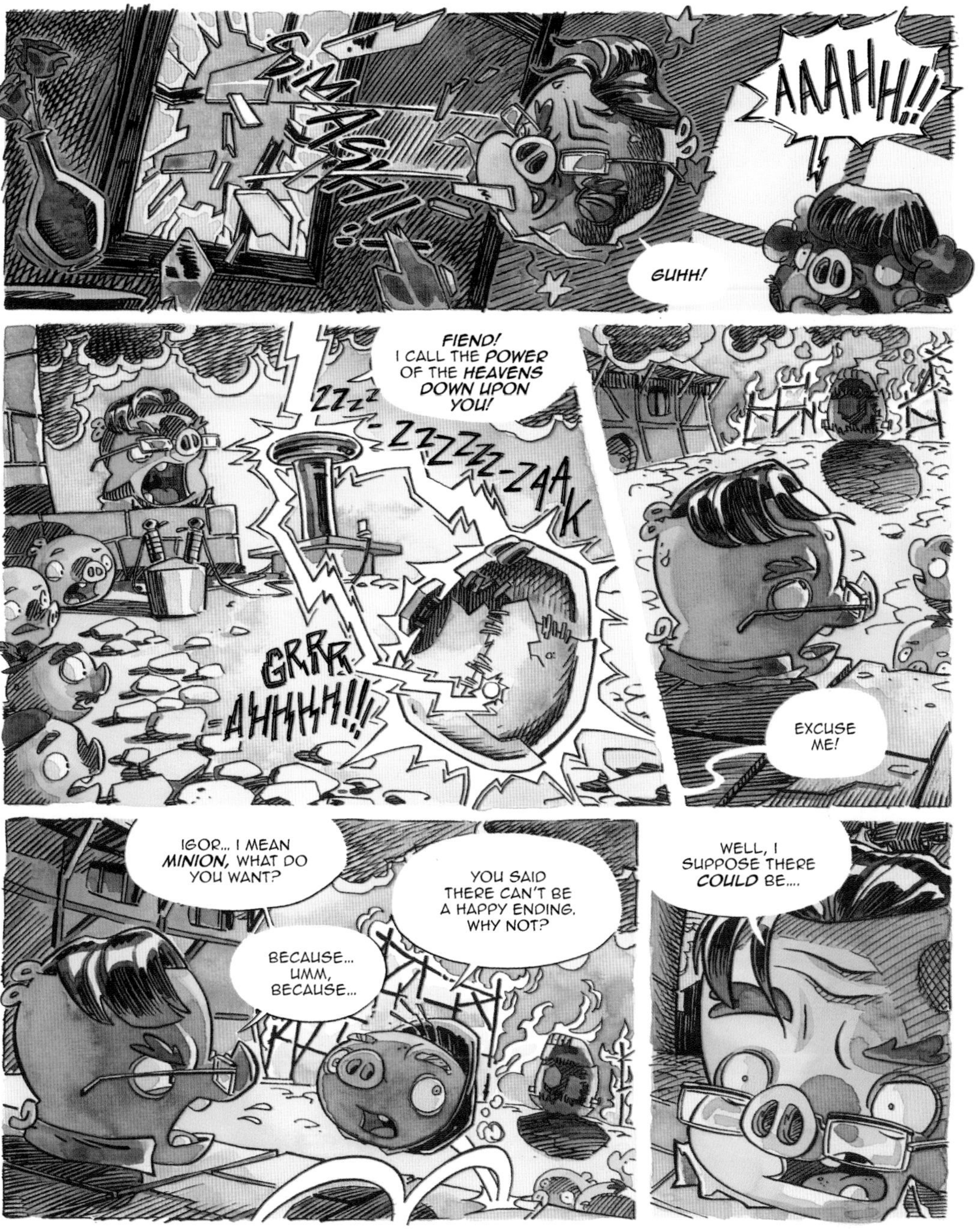
SMASH!
AAAHH!!
GUHH!
FIEND! I CALL THE POWER OF THE HEAVENS DOWN UPON YOU!
ZZzz
ZZZZZZ-ZAAK
GRRRR AHHHH!!!
EXCUSE ME!
IGOR... I MEAN MINION, WHAT DO YOU WANT?
YOU SAID THERE CAN'T BE A HAPPY ENDING. WHY NOT?
BECAUSE... UMM, BECAUSE...
WELL, I SUPPOSE THERE COULD BE....

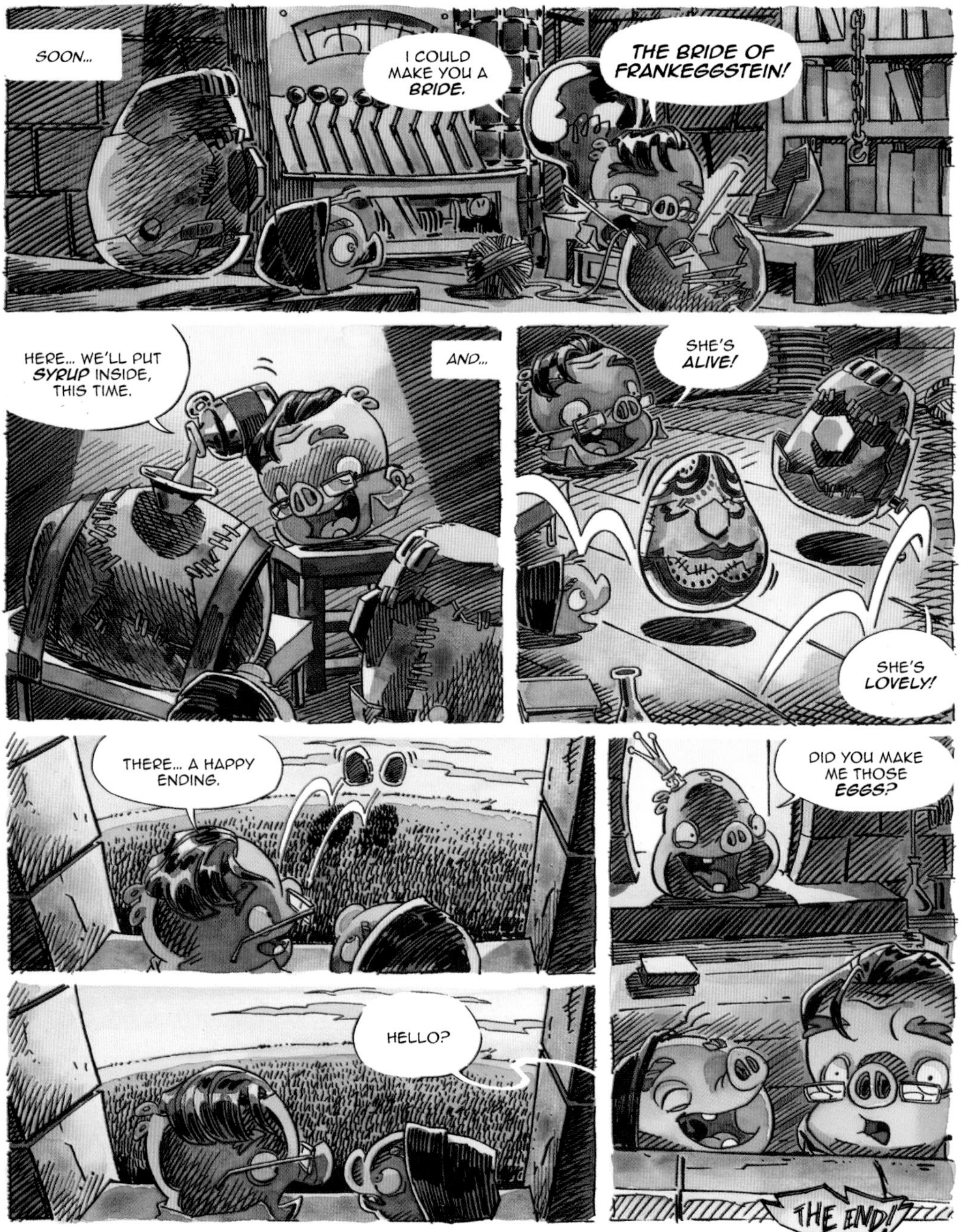
SOON...
I COULD MAKE YOU A BRIDE.
THE BRIDE OF FRANKEGGSTEIN!
HERE... WE'LL PUT SYRUP INSIDE, THIS TIME.
AND...
SHE'S ALIVE!
SHE'S LOVELY!
THERE... A HAPPY ENDING.
HELLO?
DID YOU MAKE ME THOSE EGGS?
THE END!

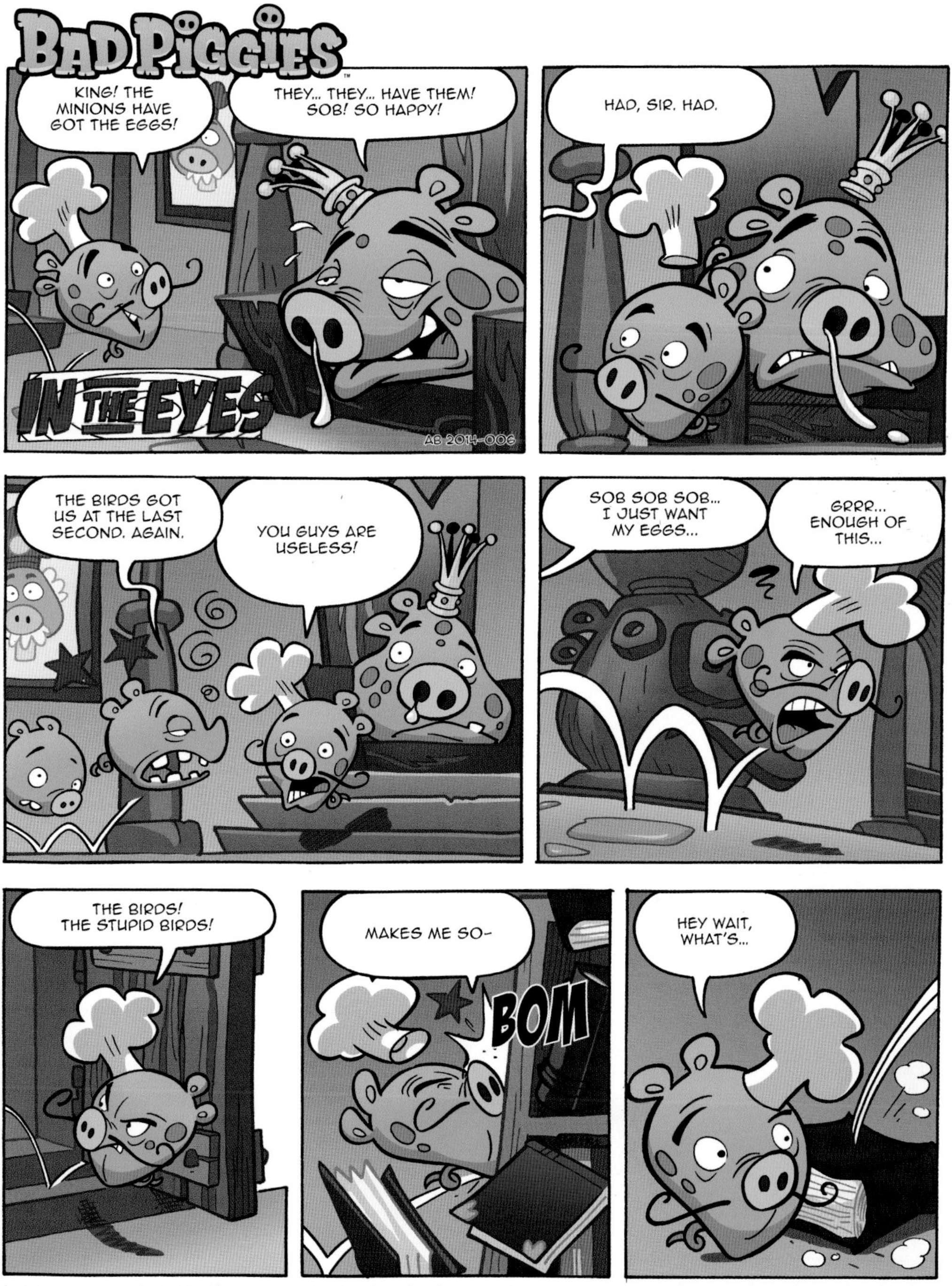
BAD PIGGIES™
KING! THE MINIONS HAVE GOT THE EGGS!
THEY... THEY... HAVE THEM! SOB! SO HAPPY!
IN THE EYES
AB 2014-006
HAD, SIR. HAD.
THE BIRDS GOT US AT THE LAST SECOND. AGAIN.
YOU GUYS ARE USELESS!
SOB SOB SOB... I JUST WANT MY EGGS...
GRRR... ENOUGH OF THIS...
THE BIRDS! THE STUPID BIRDS!
MAKES ME SO-
BOM
HEY WAIT, WHAT'S...

WRITTEN BY: FRANÇOIS CORTEGGIANI • ART BY: GIORGIO CAVAZZANO WITH A. ZEMOLIN
COLORS BY: DIGIKORE • LETTERS BY: PISARA OY

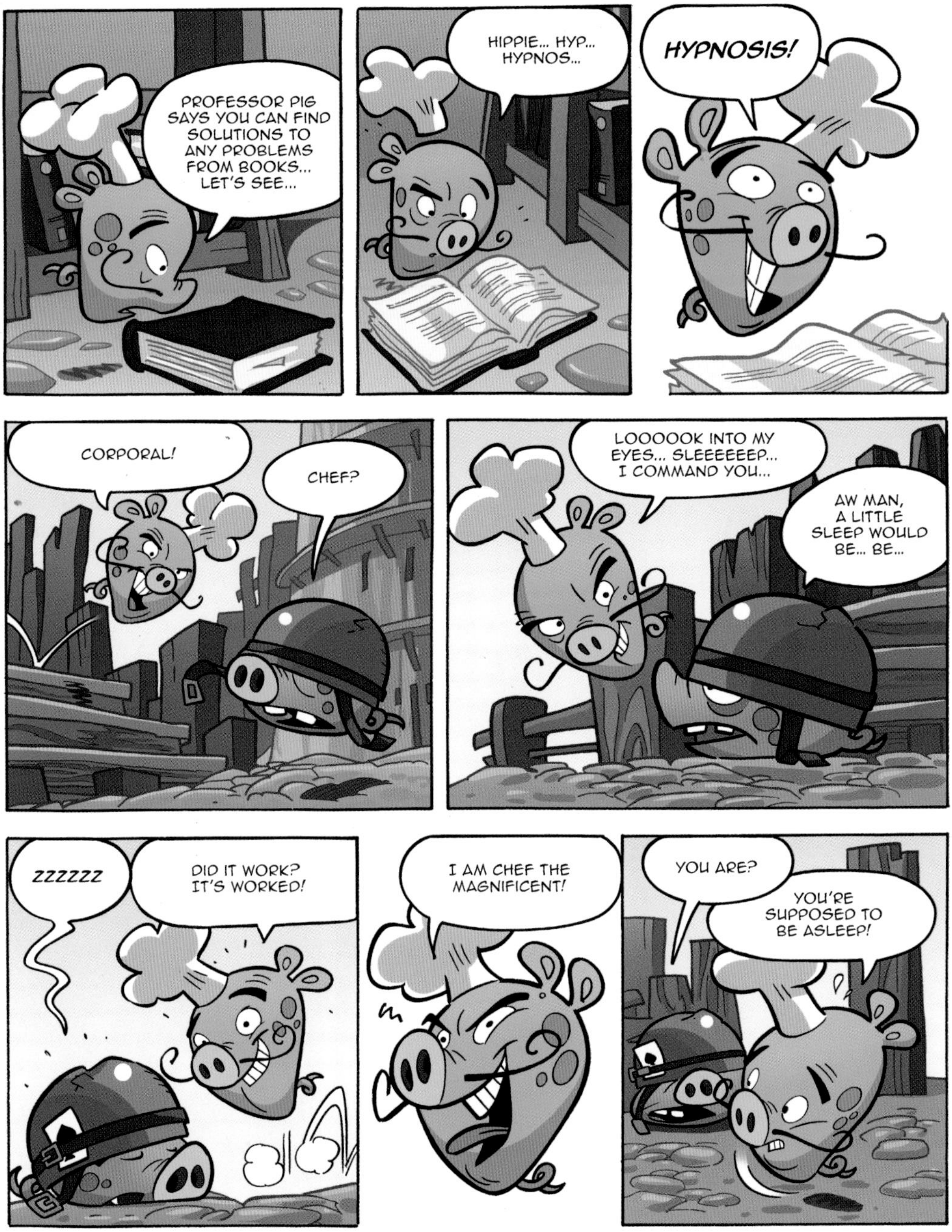
PROFESSOR PIG SAYS YOU CAN FIND SOLUTIONS TO ANY PROBLEMS FROM BOOKS... LET'S SEE...
HIPPIE... HYP... HYPNOS...
HYPNOSIS!
CORPORAL!
CHEF?
LOOOOOK INTO MY EYES... SLEEEEEEP... I COMMAND YOU...
AW MAN, A LITTLE SLEEP WOULD BE... BE...
ZZZZZZ
DID IT WORK? IT'S WORKED!
I AM CHEF THE MAGNIFICENT!
YOU ARE?
YOU'RE SUPPOSED TO BE ASLEEP!

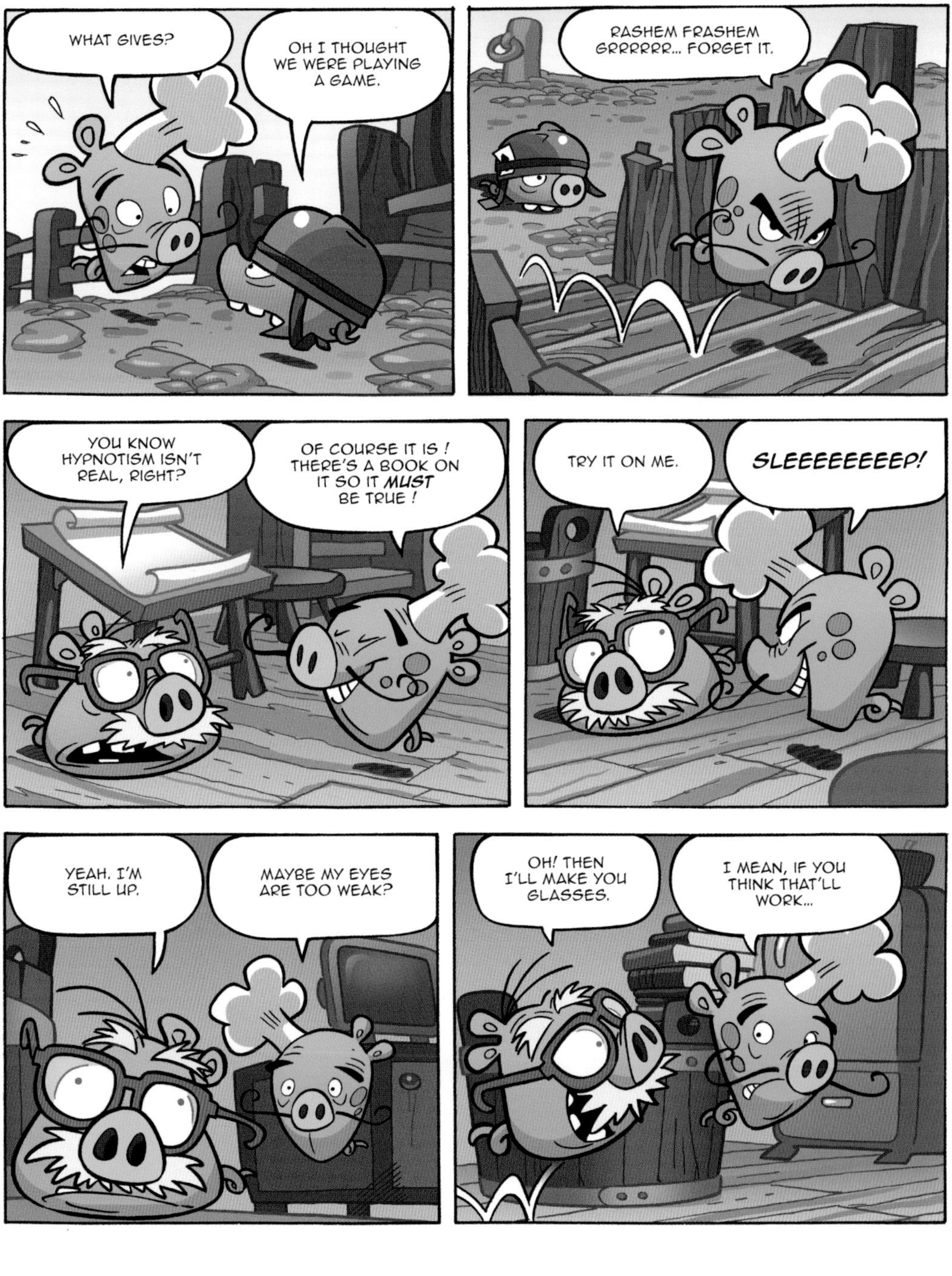
WHAT GIVES?
OH I THOUGHT WE WERE PLAYING A GAME.
RASHEM FRASHEM GRRRRRR... FORGET IT.
YOU KNOW HYPNOTISM ISN'T REAL, RIGHT?
OF COURSE IT IS ! THERE'S A BOOK ON IT SO IT MUST BE TRUE !
TRY IT ON ME.
SLEEEEEEEEEP!
YEAH. I'M STILL UP.
MAYBE MY EYES ARE TOO WEAK?
OH! THEN I'LL MAKE YOU GLASSES.
I MEAN, IF YOU THINK THAT'LL WORK...

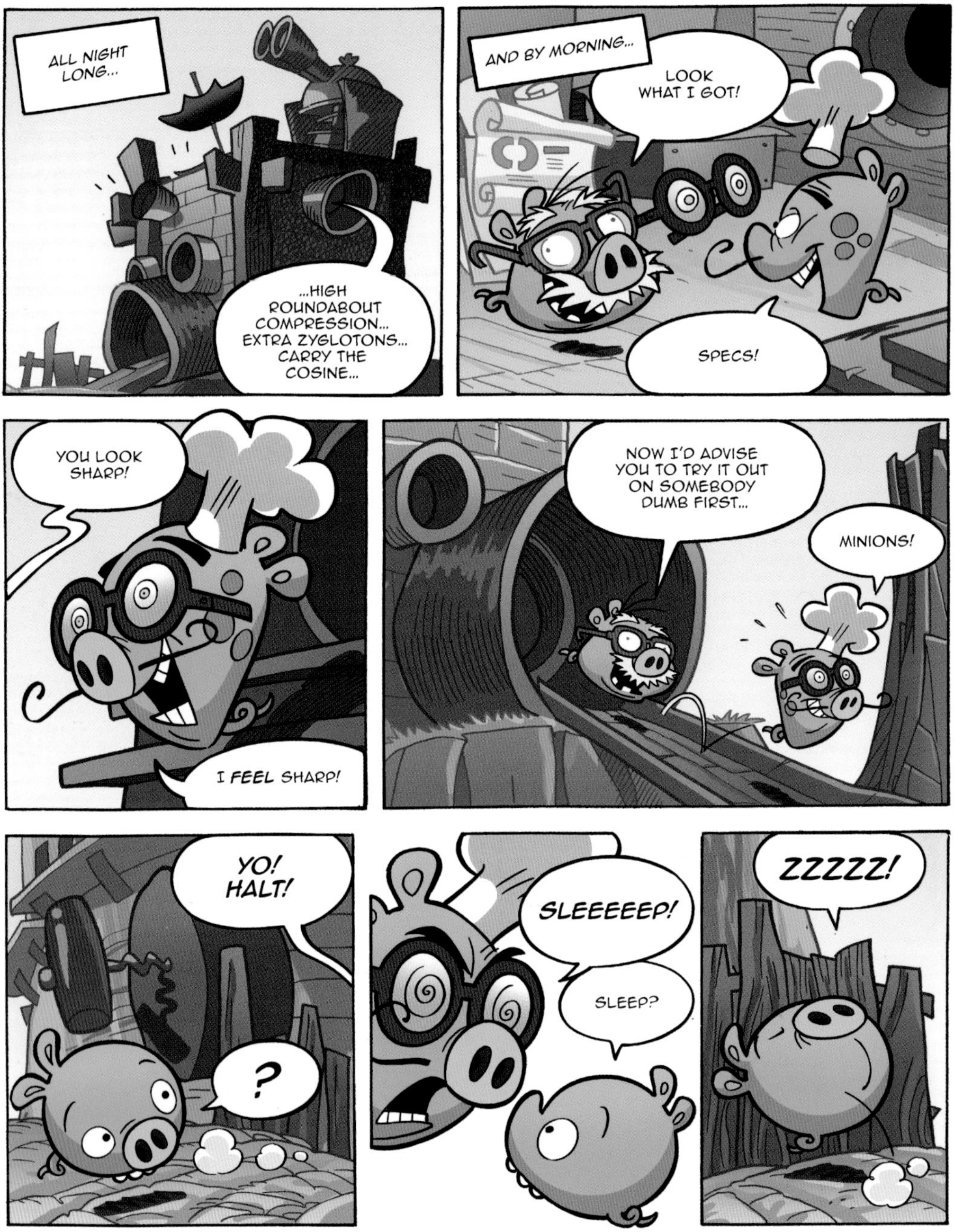
ALL NIGHT LONG...
...HIGH ROUNDABOUT COMPRESSION... EXTRA ZYGLOTONS... CARRY THE COSINE...
AND BY MORNING...
LOOK WHAT I GOT!
SPECS!
YOU LOOK SHARP!
I FEEL SHARP!
NOW I'D ADVISE YOU TO TRY IT OUT ON SOMEBODY DUMB FIRST...
MINIONS!
YO! HALT!
?
SLEEEEEP!
SLEEP?
ZZZZZ!

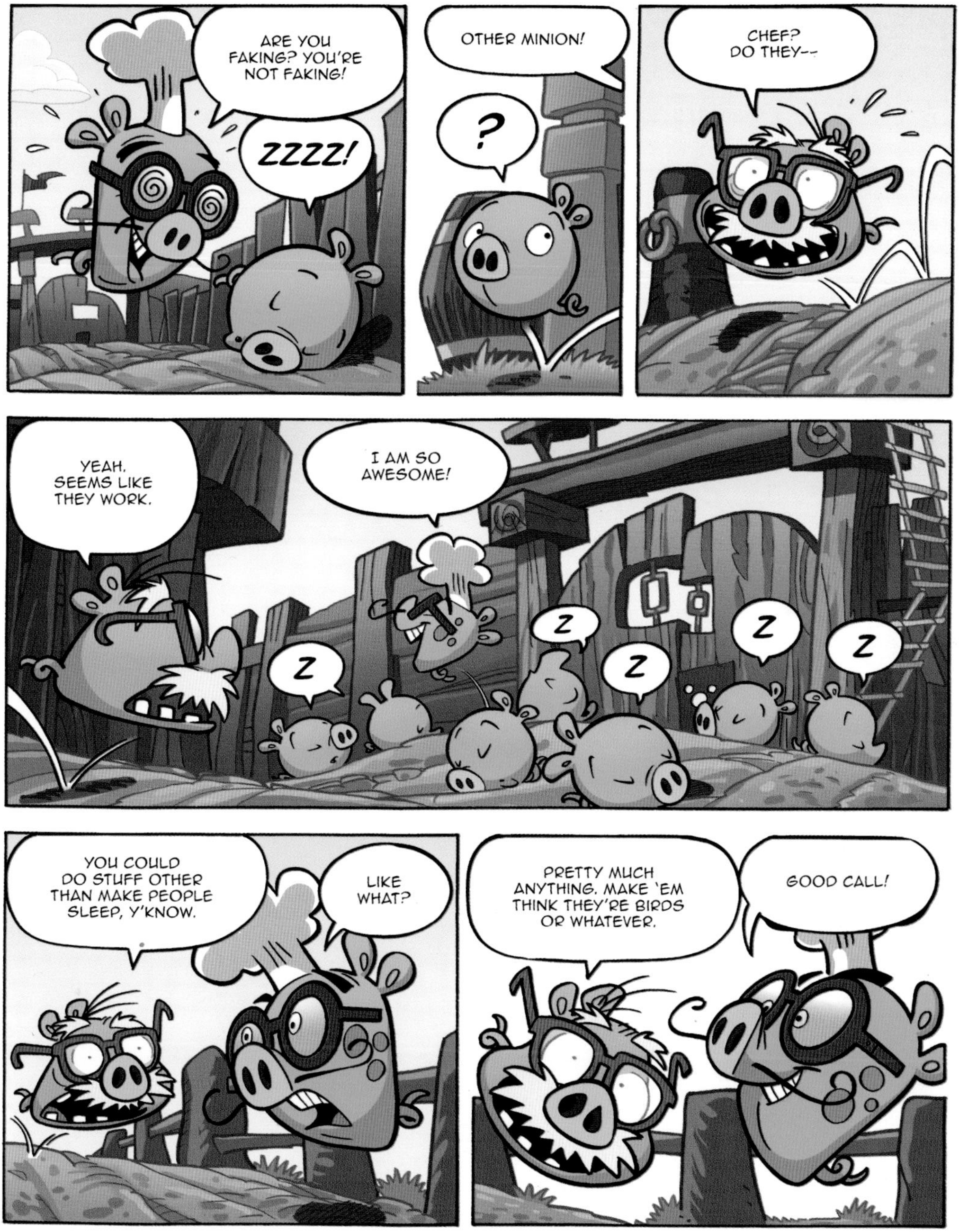
ARE YOU FAKING? YOU'RE NOT FAKING!
ZZZZ!
OTHER MINION!
?
CHEF? DO THEY--
YEAH. SEEMS LIKE THEY WORK.
I AM SO AWESOME!
Z
Z
Z
Z
Z
YOU COULD DO STUFF OTHER THAN MAKE PEOPLE SLEEP, Y'KNOW.
LIKE WHAT?
PRETTY MUCH ANYTHING. MAKE 'EM THINK THEY'RE BIRDS OR WHATEVER.
GOOD CALL!

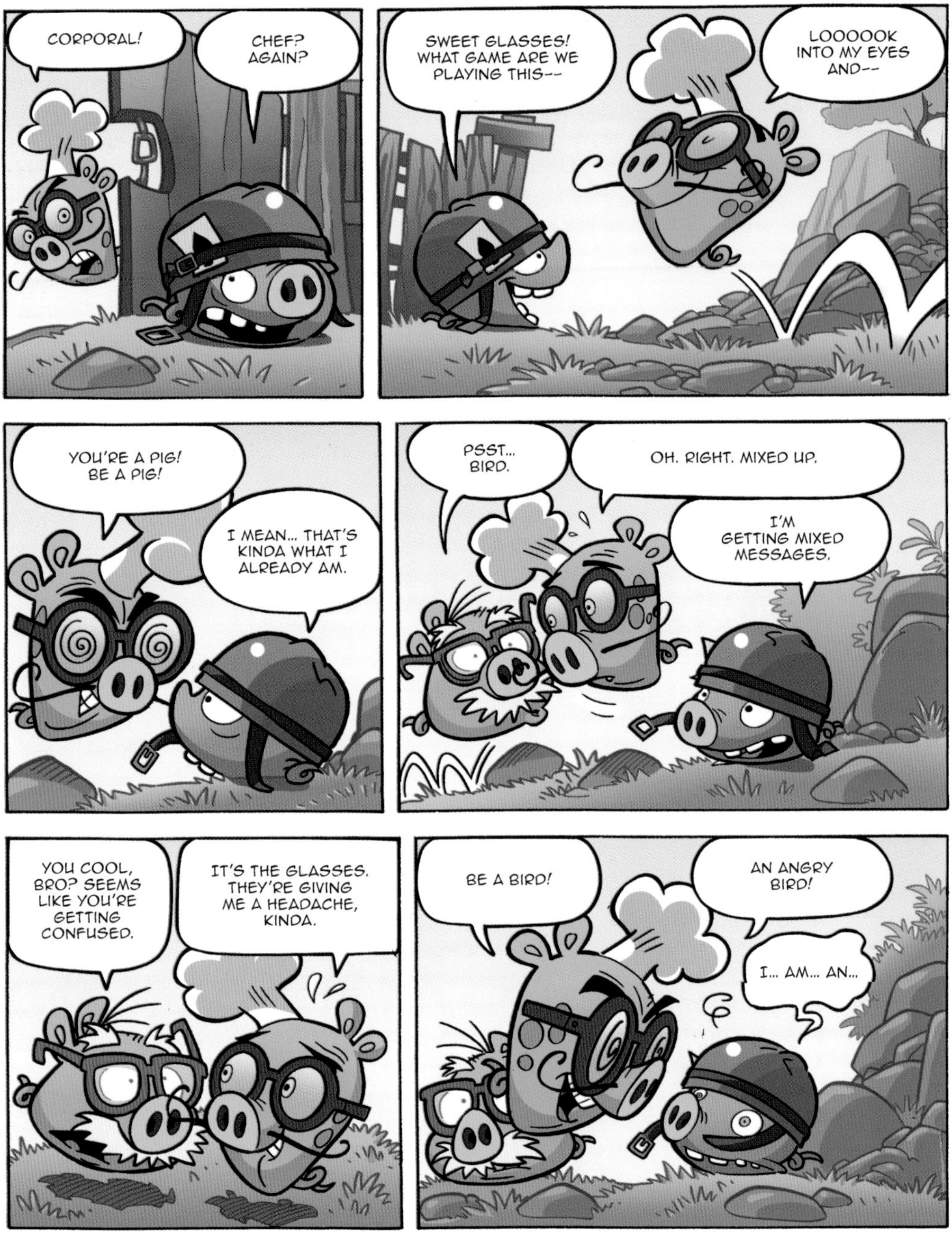
CORPORAL!
CHEF? AGAIN?
SWEET GLASSES! WHAT GAME ARE WE PLAYING THIS--
LOOOOOK INTO MY EYES AND--
YOU'RE A PIG! BE A PIG!
I MEAN... THAT'S KINDA WHAT I ALREADY AM.
PSST... BIRD.
OH. RIGHT. MIXED UP.
I'M GETTING MIXED MESSAGES.
YOU COOL, BRO? SEEMS LIKE YOU'RE GETTING CONFUSED.
IT'S THE GLASSES. THEY'RE GIVING ME A HEADACHE, KINDA.
BE A BIRD!
AN ANGRY BIRD!
I... AM... AN...

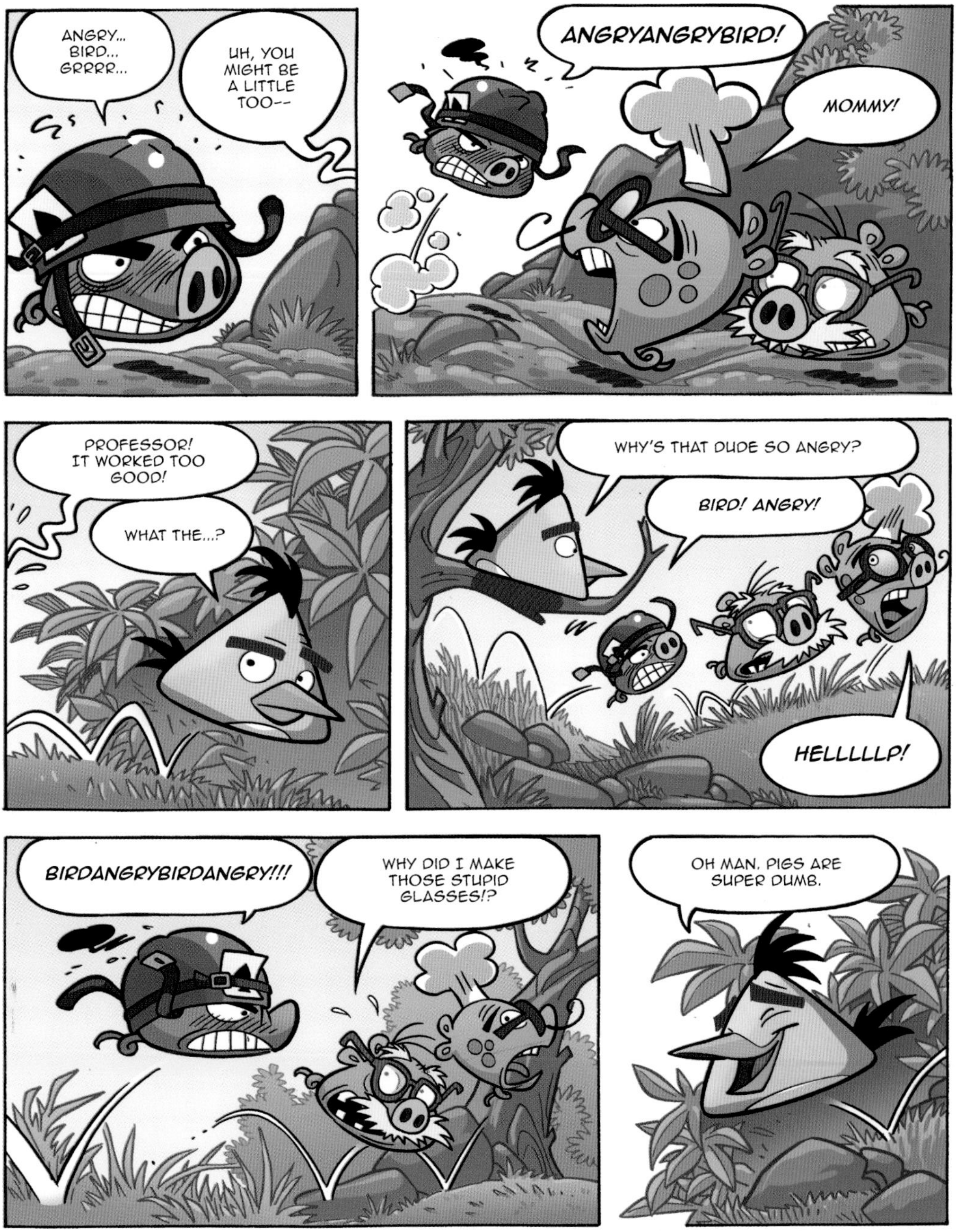

ANGRY... BIRD... GRRRR...
UH, YOU MIGHT BE A LITTLE TOO--
ANGRYANGRYBIRD!
MOMMY!
PROFESSOR! IT WORKED TOO GOOD!
WHAT THE...?
WHY'S THAT DUDE SO ANGRY?
BIRD! ANGRY!
HELLLLLP!
BIRDANGRYBIRDANGRY!!!
WHY DID I MAKE THOSE STUPID GLASSES!?
OH MAN. PIGS ARE SUPER DUMB.

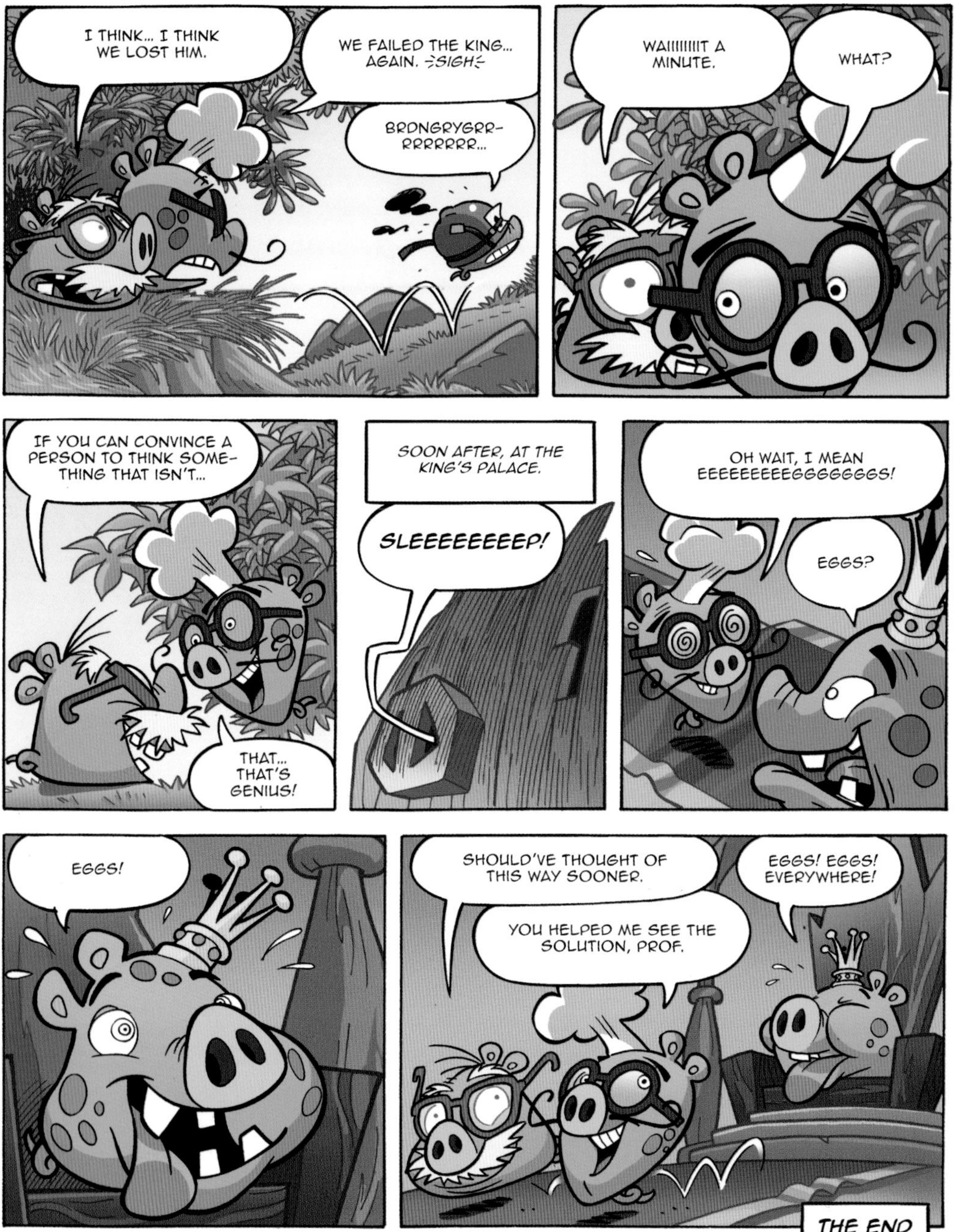
I THINK... I THINK WE LOST HIM.
WE FAILED THE KING... AGAIN. ~SIGH~
BRDNGRYGRR-RRRRRRR...
WAIIIIIIIT A MINUTE.
WHAT?
IF YOU CAN CONVINCE A PERSON TO THINK SOME-THING THAT ISN'T...
THAT... THAT'S GENIUS!
SOON AFTER, AT THE KING'S PALACE.
SLEEEEEEEEP!
OH WAIT, I MEAN EEEEEEEEEGGGGGGGS!
EGGS?
EGGS!
SHOULD'VE THOUGHT OF THIS WAY SOONER.
YOU HELPED ME SEE THE SOLUTION, PROF.
EGGS! EGGS! EVERYWHERE!
THE END

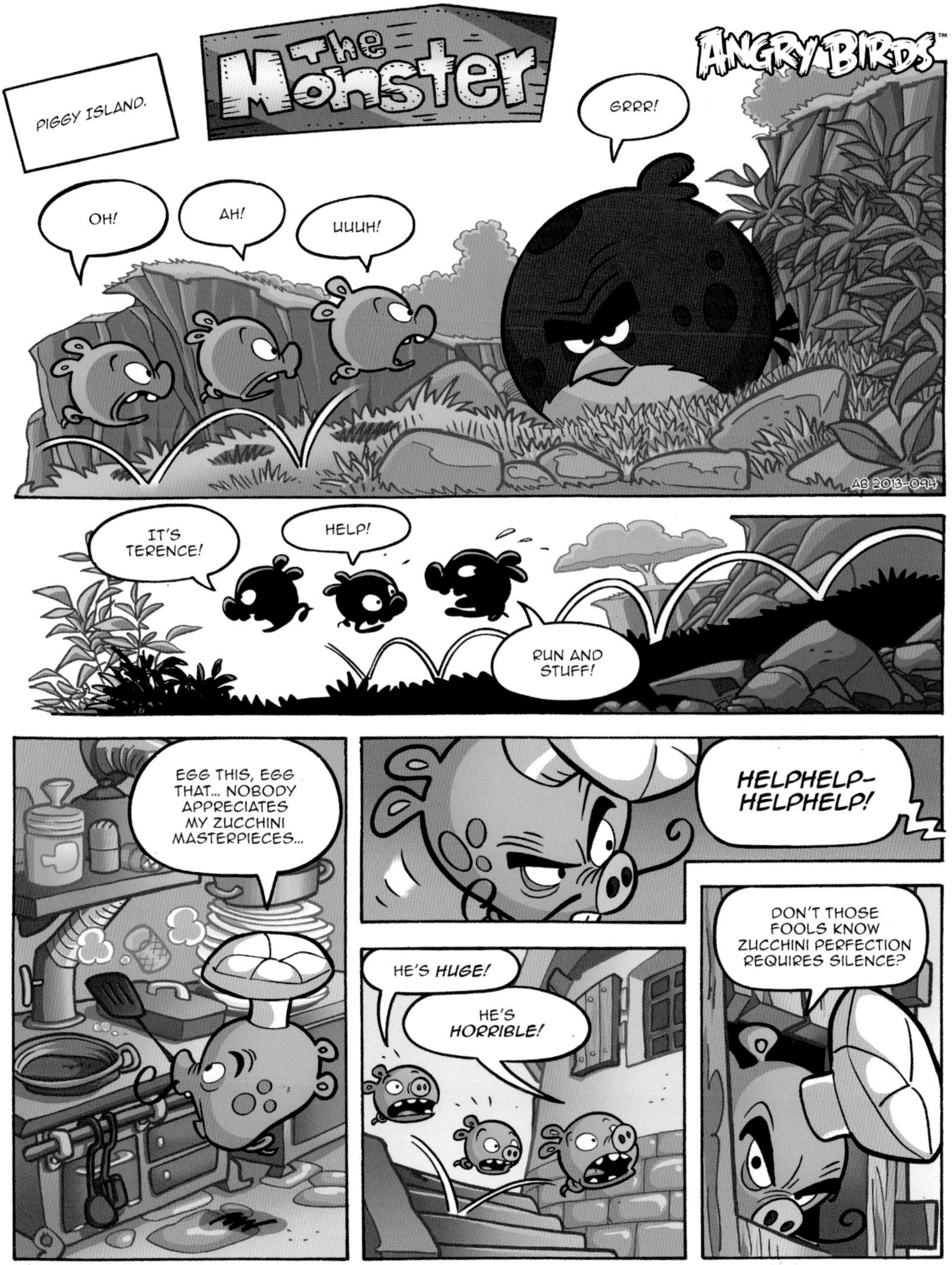
The Monster
ANGRY BIRDS
PIGGY ISLAND.
GRRR!
OH!
AH!
UUUH!
AB 2013-094
IT'S TERENCE!
HELP!
RUN AND STUFF!
EGG THIS, EGG THAT... NOBODY APPRECIATES MY ZUCCHINI MASTERPIECES...
HELPHELP-HELPHELP!
HE'S *HUGE!*
HE'S *HORRIBLE!*
DON'T THOSE FOOLS KNOW ZUCCHINI PERFECTION REQUIRES SILENCE?

WRITTEN BY: FRANÇOIS CORTEGGIANI • ART BY: GIORGIO CAVAZZANO • COLORS BY: DIGIKORE • LETTERS BY: PISARA OY

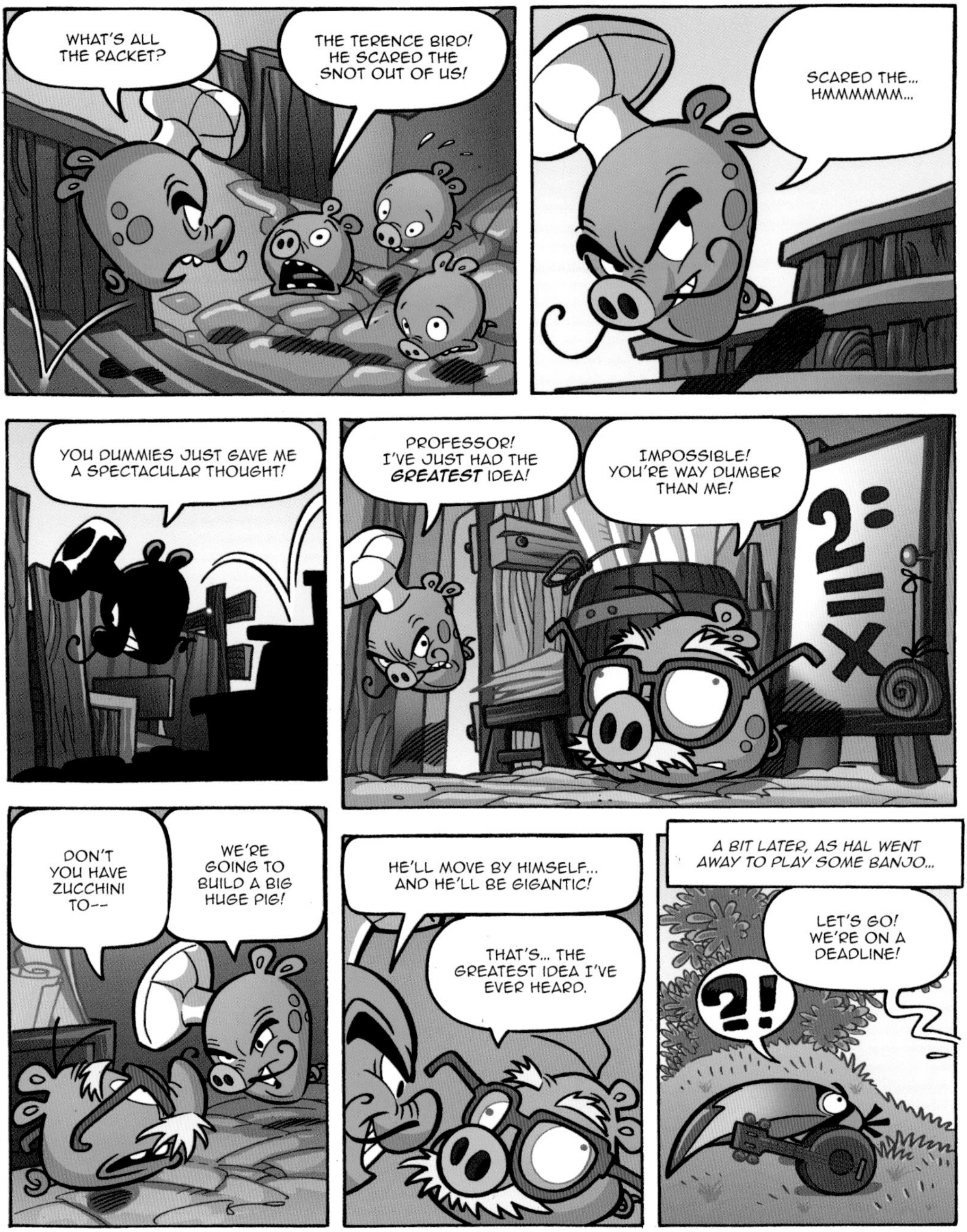
WHAT'S ALL THE RACKET?
THE TERENCE BIRD! HE SCARED THE SNOT OUT OF US!
SCARED THE... HMMMMMM...
YOU DUMMIES JUST GAVE ME A SPECTACULAR THOUGHT!
PROFESSOR! I'VE JUST HAD THE GREATEST IDEA!
IMPOSSIBLE! YOU'RE WAY DUMBER THAN ME!
DON'T YOU HAVE ZUCCHINI TO--
WE'RE GOING TO BUILD A BIG HUGE PIG!
HE'LL MOVE BY HIMSELF... AND HE'LL BE GIGANTIC!
THAT'S... THE GREATEST IDEA I'VE EVER HEARD.
A BIT LATER, AS HAL WENT AWAY TO PLAY SOME BANJO...
LET'S GO! WE'RE ON A DEADLINE!
?!

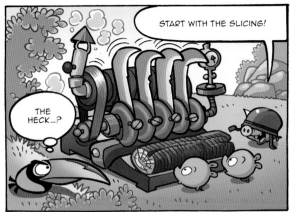

START WITH THE SLICING!

THE HECK...?

WHEELS DONE! LET'S GET THESE BACK TO THE CASTLE!

BETTER WARN RED ABOUT... WHATEVER THIS IS...

WHEELS? FOR WHAT?

DUNNO. THAT'S WHY I'M TELLING YOU, BOSS BIRD!

I'LL USE MY INCREDIBLE SNEAKING ABILITIES TO FIGURE THIS OUT!

THAT EVENING...

SNEEEEAK SNEAK SNEAKITY SNEAK...

OOOOOHMIGOSH!

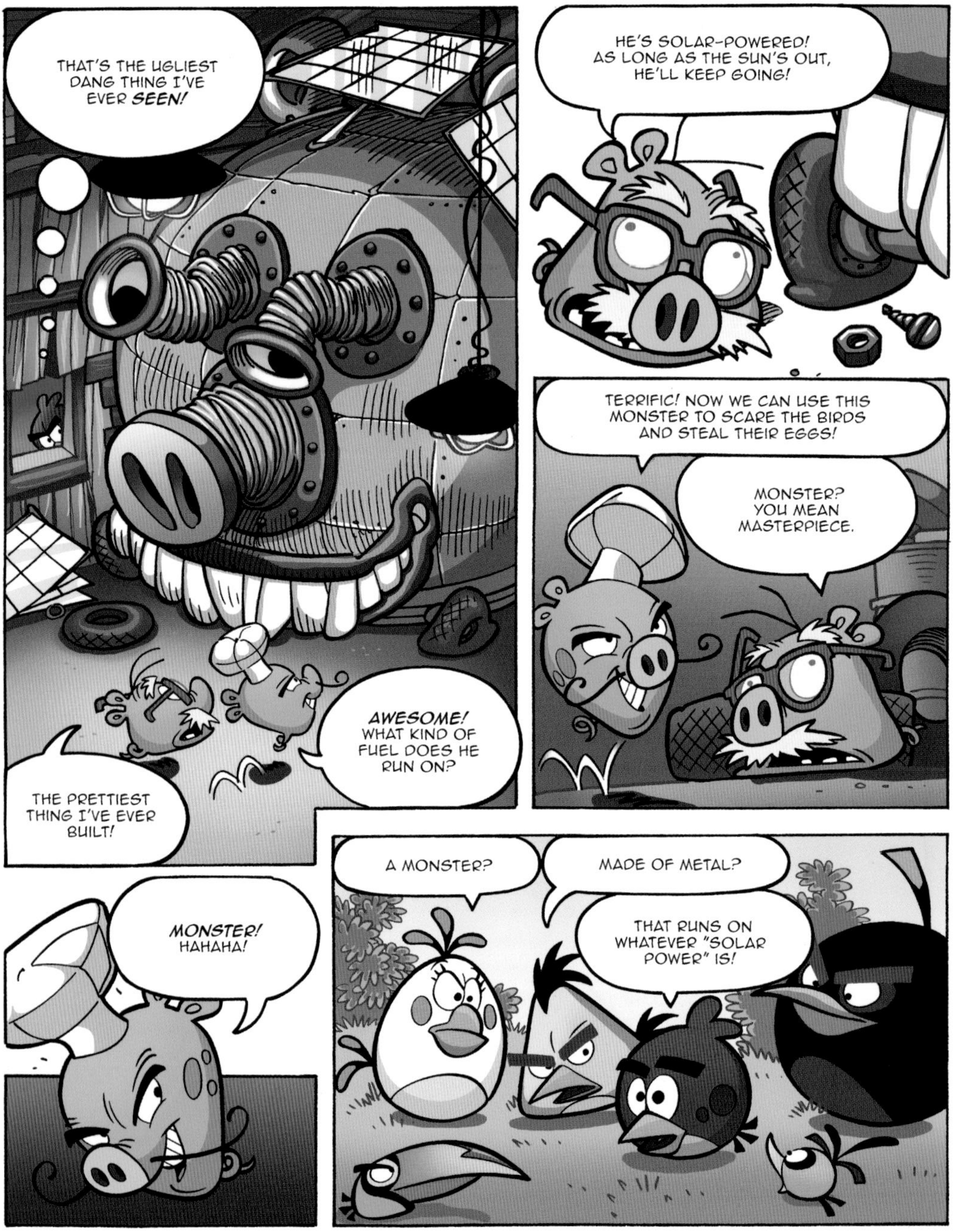
THAT'S THE UGLIEST DANG THING I'VE EVER SEEN!
THE PRETTIEST THING I'VE EVER BUILT!
AWESOME! WHAT KIND OF FUEL DOES HE RUN ON?
HE'S SOLAR-POWERED! AS LONG AS THE SUN'S OUT, HE'LL KEEP GOING!
TERRIFIC! NOW WE CAN USE THIS MONSTER TO SCARE THE BIRDS AND STEAL THEIR EGGS!
MONSTER? YOU MEAN MASTERPIECE.
MONSTER! HAHAHA!
A MONSTER?
MADE OF METAL?
THAT RUNS ON WHATEVER "SOLAR POWER" IS!

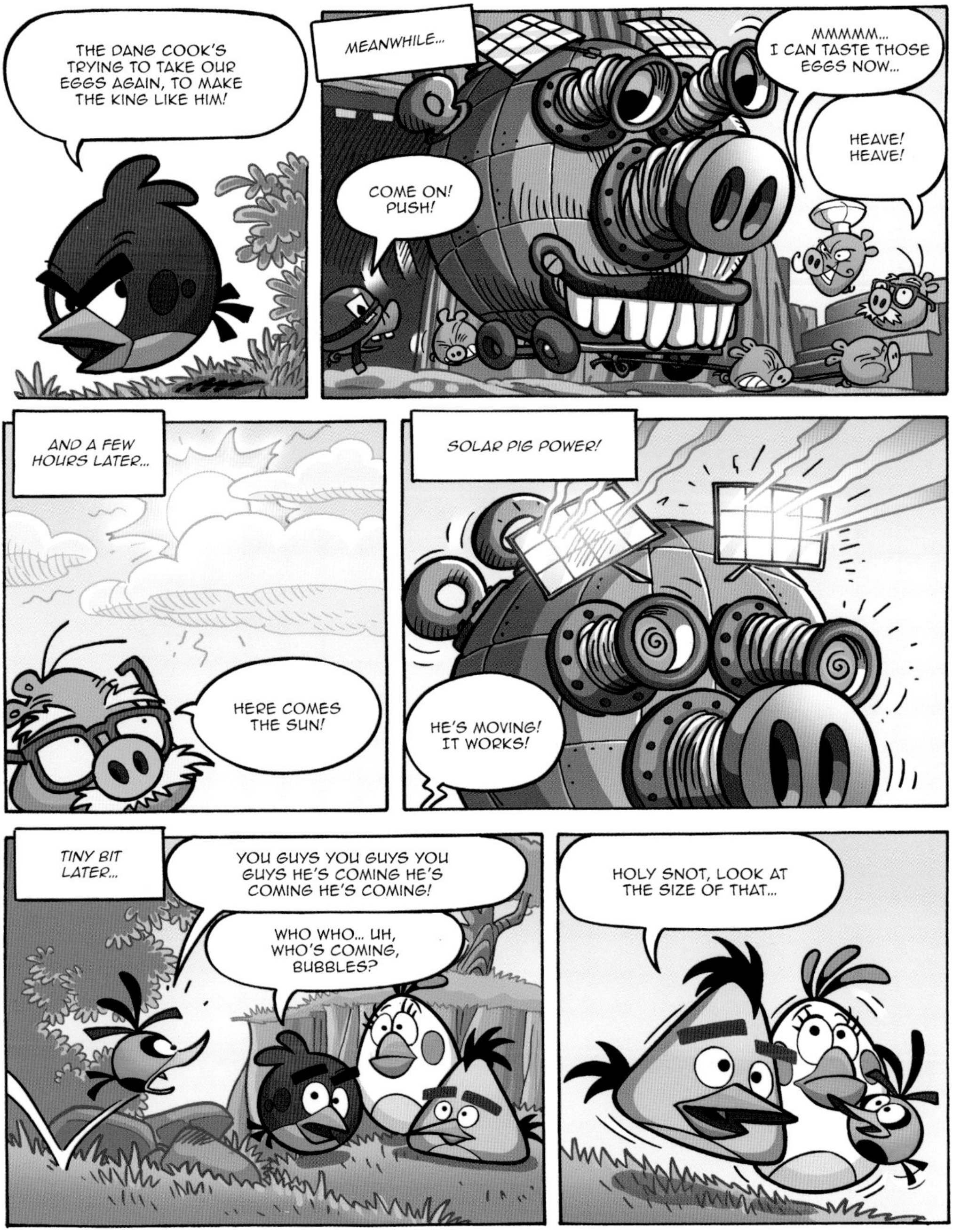
THE DANG COOK'S TRYING TO TAKE OUR EGGS AGAIN, TO MAKE THE KING LIKE HIM!
MEANWHILE...
MMMMM... I CAN TASTE THOSE EGGS NOW...
HEAVE! HEAVE!
COME ON! PUSH!
AND A FEW HOURS LATER...
HERE COMES THE SUN!
SOLAR PIG POWER!
HE'S MOVING! IT WORKS!
TINY BIT LATER...
YOU GUYS YOU GUYS YOU GUYS HE'S COMING HE'S COMING HE'S COMING!
WHO WHO... UH, WHO'S COMING, BUBBLES?
HOLY SNOT, LOOK AT THE SIZE OF THAT...

PIG!
SCATTER! CHUCK, BUBBLES YOU'RE WITH ME!
AAH!
RUN!
HAL! WE NEED YOU!
TERENCE! MEET US AT THE SLING!
?
A FEW SECONDS LATER...
MMF, READY?
ROGER THAT! RELEASE!
WOOOOOOOO!
BRACE FOR IMPACT!

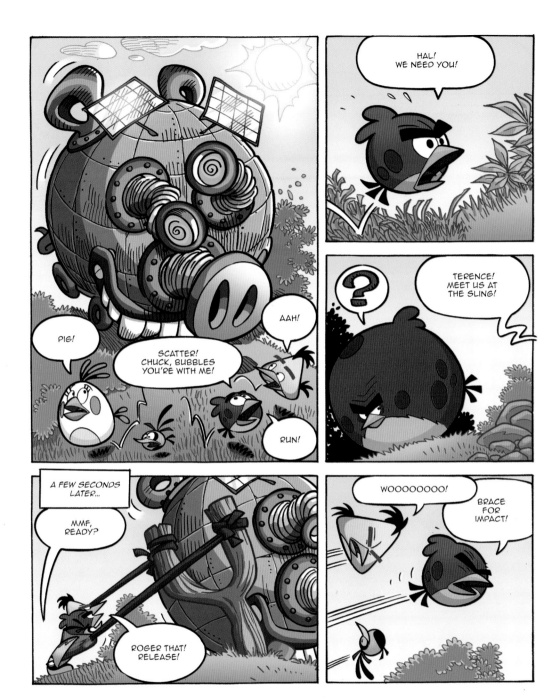

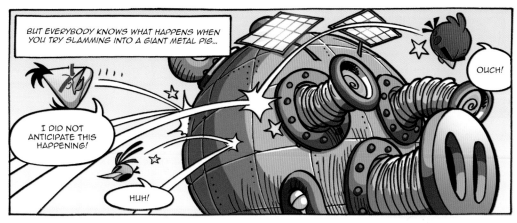

BUT EVERYBODY KNOWS WHAT HAPPENS WHEN YOU TRY SLAMMING INTO A GIANT METAL PIG...

OUCH!

I DID NOT ANTICIPATE THIS HAPPENING!

HUH!

THE DUDE'S TOO BIG AND METAL! WE'VE GOT TO THINK OF ANOTHER STRATEGY...

LET'S GO WITH THE TERENCE STRATEGY!

UGH!

WE CAN'T MAKE A DENT, AND THE SUN'S GONNA KEEP HIM POWERED FOREVER!

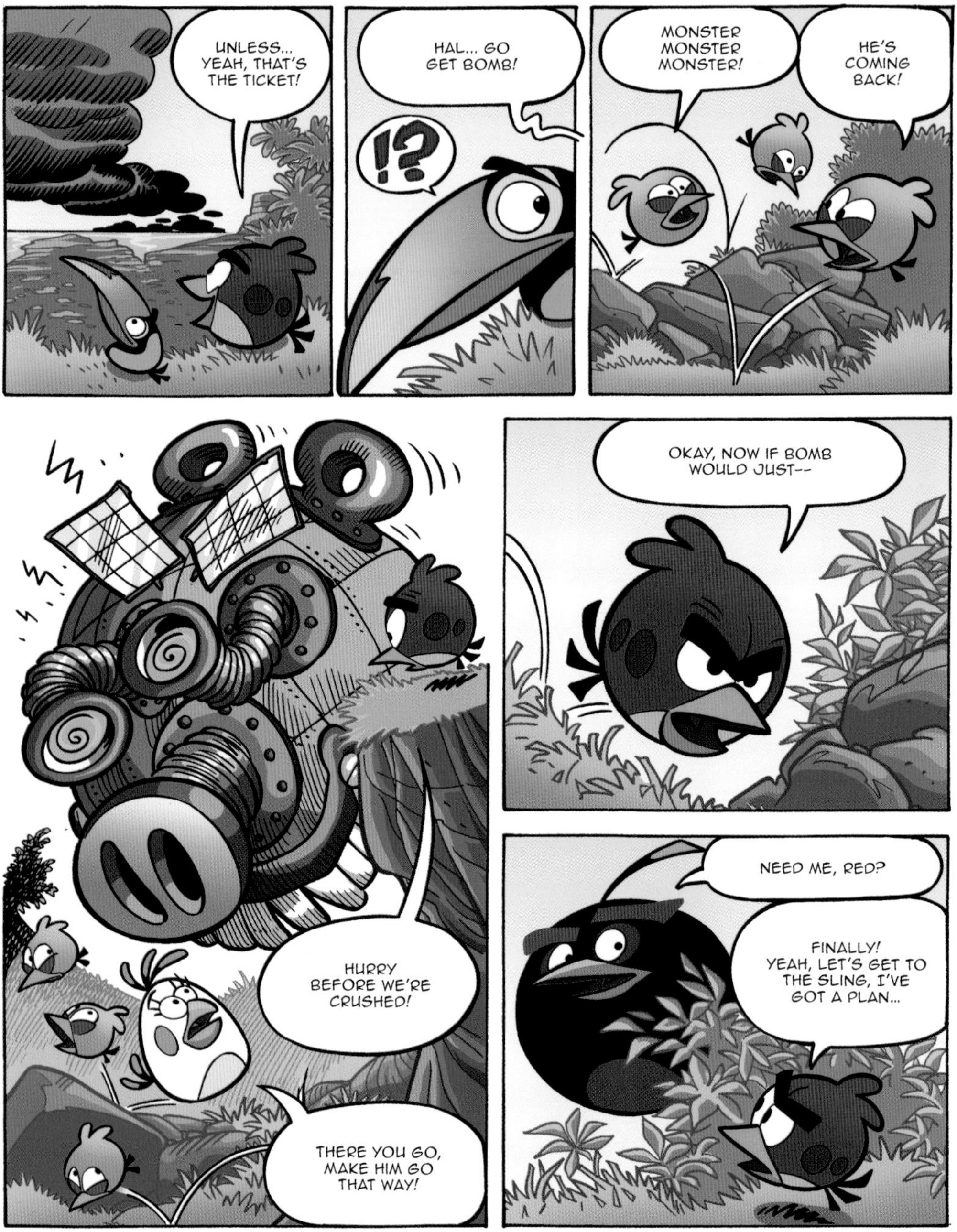
UNLESS... YEAH, THAT'S THE TICKET!
HAL... GO GET BOMB!
!?
MONSTER MONSTER MONSTER!
HE'S COMING BACK!
HURRY BEFORE WE'RE CRUSHED!
THERE YOU GO, MAKE HIM GO THAT WAY!
OKAY, NOW IF BOMB WOULD JUST--
NEED ME, RED?
FINALLY! YEAH, LET'S GET TO THE SLING, I'VE GOT A PLAN...

AND SOON AFTER...

AWRIGHT, THE CLOUDS ARE STARTING TO BLOCK THE SUN! YOU'RE UP BOMB!

YAAAAH!

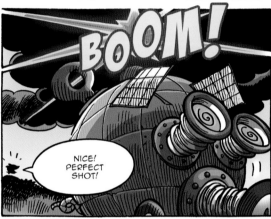

BOOM!

NICE! PERFECT SHOT!

SIZZLE!

BZZZT!

THE SUN IS WHAT GAVE THE METAL PIG POWER! BUT LIGHTNING? NOT SO MUCH!

HE'S GONNA BLOW!

TAKE COVER! METAL HURTS WHEN IT BLOWS UP!

CRAC-A-BOOM!!!

DOES IT HAVE THE EGGS? DID WE WIN?

I CAN TASTE THE VICTORY NOW! LOOKS LIKE HE'S THROWN THE EGGS IN OUR DIRECTION!

THROWN? I DIDN'T PROGRAM HIM TO DO THAT.

THEN WHAT'S...?

AGGGH!

THAT'S GONNA LEAVE A MARK!

DAY SAVED, TERENCE! HOW'S IT FEEL BEING THE BIGGEST MONSTER ON THE ISLAND AGAIN?

GRMPF!

THE END

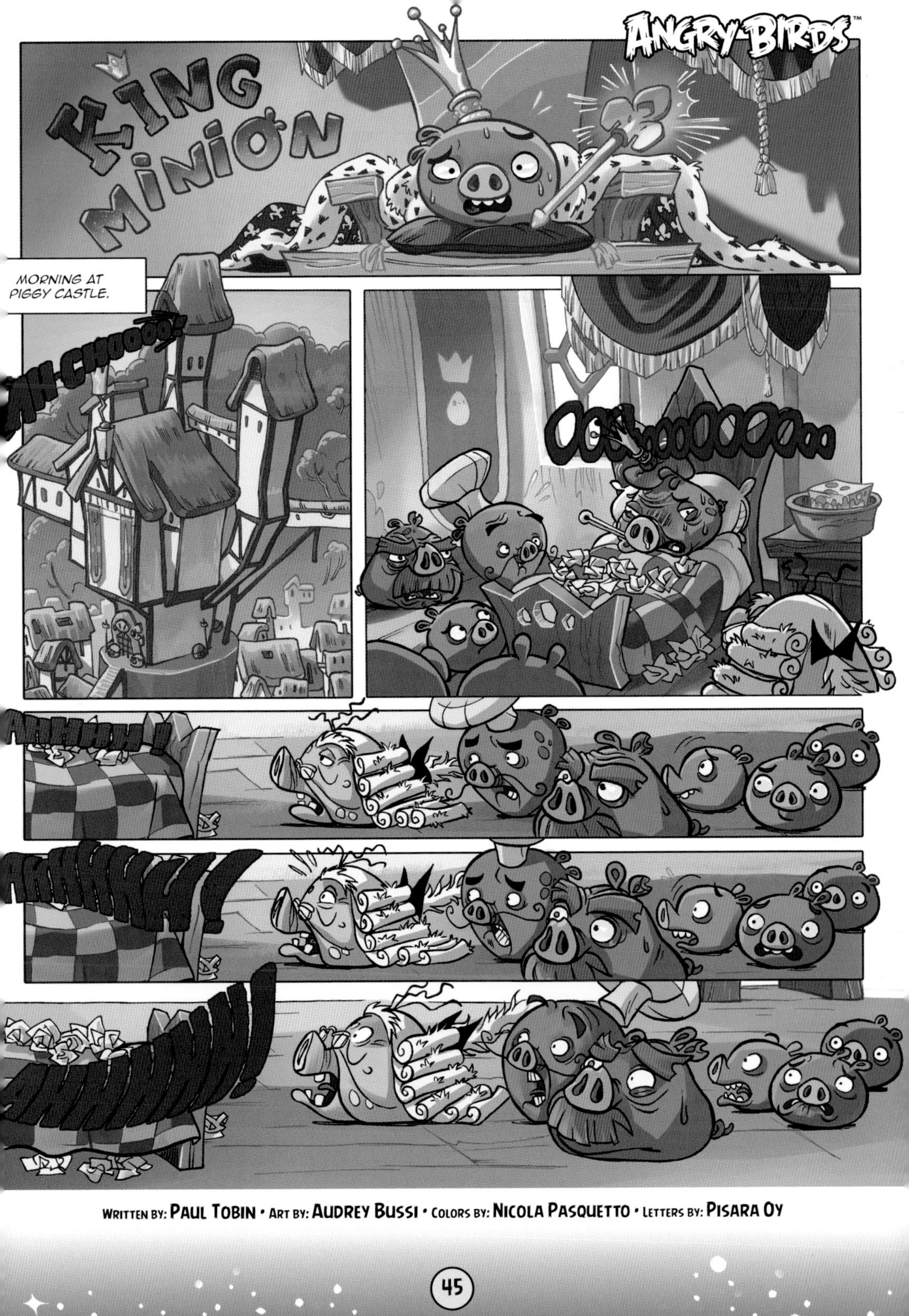
KING MINION
MORNING AT PIGGY CASTLE.
AH-CHOOOO!
OOOooOOOOooo
AHHHHH!
AHHHHHH!
AHHHHHHH!

WRITTEN BY: PAUL TOBIN • ART BY: AUDREY BUSSI • COLORS BY: NICOLA PASQUETTO • LETTERS BY: PISARA OY

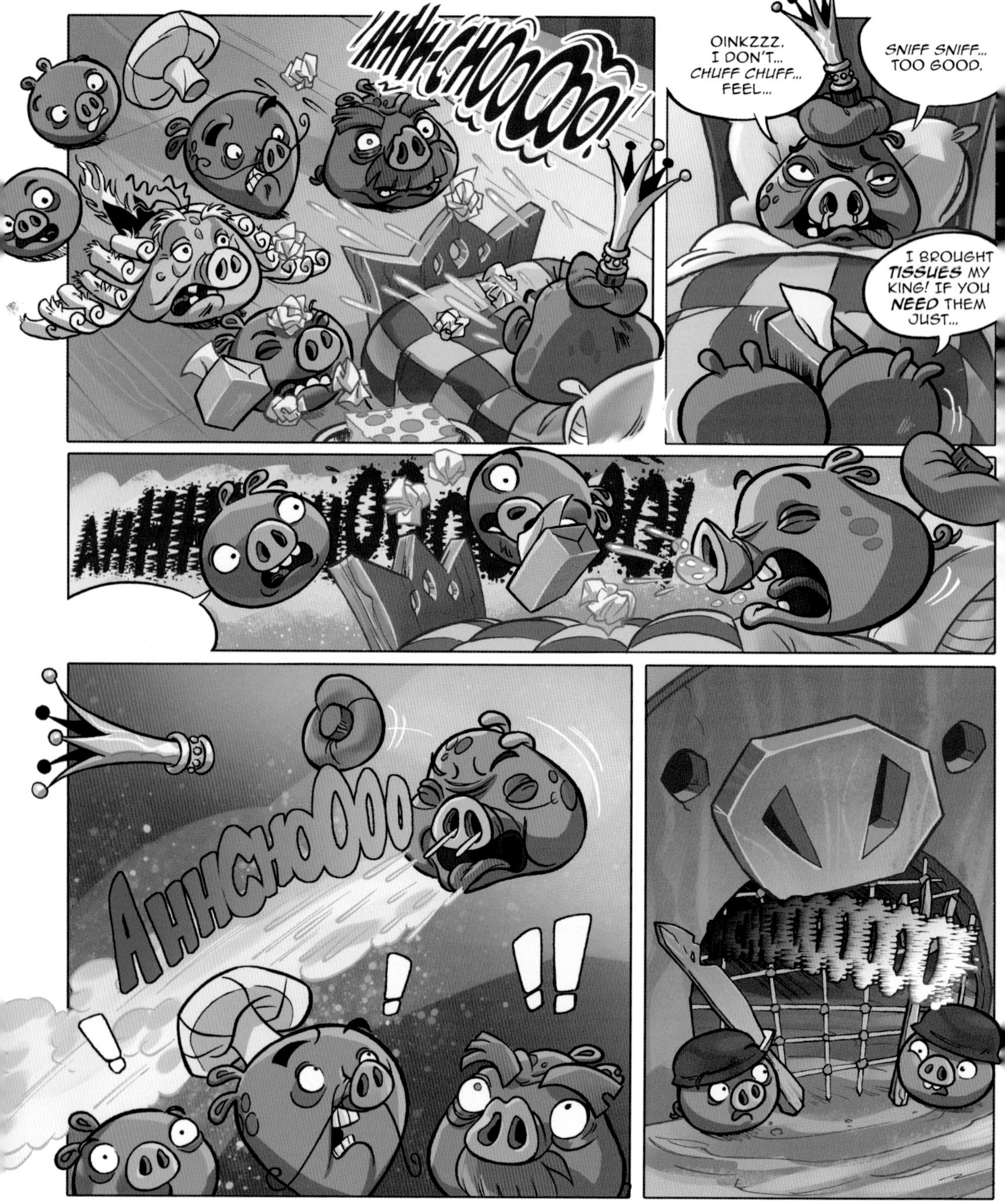
AHHH-CHOOOOO!
OINKZZZ. I DON'T... CHUFF CHUFF... FEEL...
SNIFF SNIFF... TOO GOOD.
I BROUGHT TISSUES MY KING! IF YOU NEED THEM JUST...
AHHHCHOOOO
!
!
!!

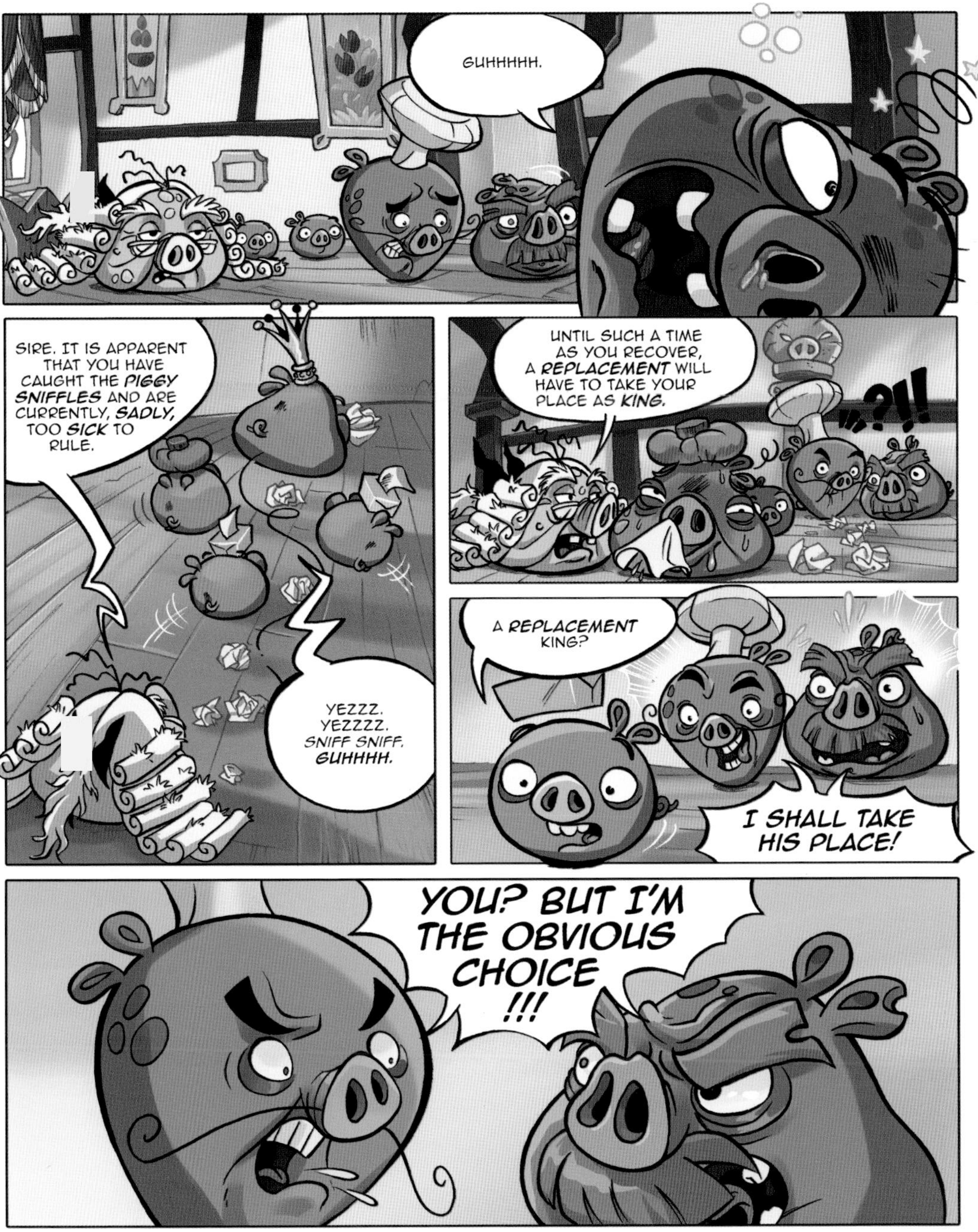
GUHHHHH.
SIRE. IT IS APPARENT THAT YOU HAVE CAUGHT THE PIGGY SNIFFLES AND ARE CURRENTLY, SADLY, TOO SICK TO RULE.
YEZZZ. YEZZZZ. SNIFF SNIFF. GUHHHH.
UNTIL SUCH A TIME AS YOU RECOVER, A REPLACEMENT WILL HAVE TO TAKE YOUR PLACE AS KING.
?!!
A REPLACEMENT KING?
I SHALL TAKE HIS PLACE!
YOU? BUT I'M THE OBVIOUS CHOICE !!!

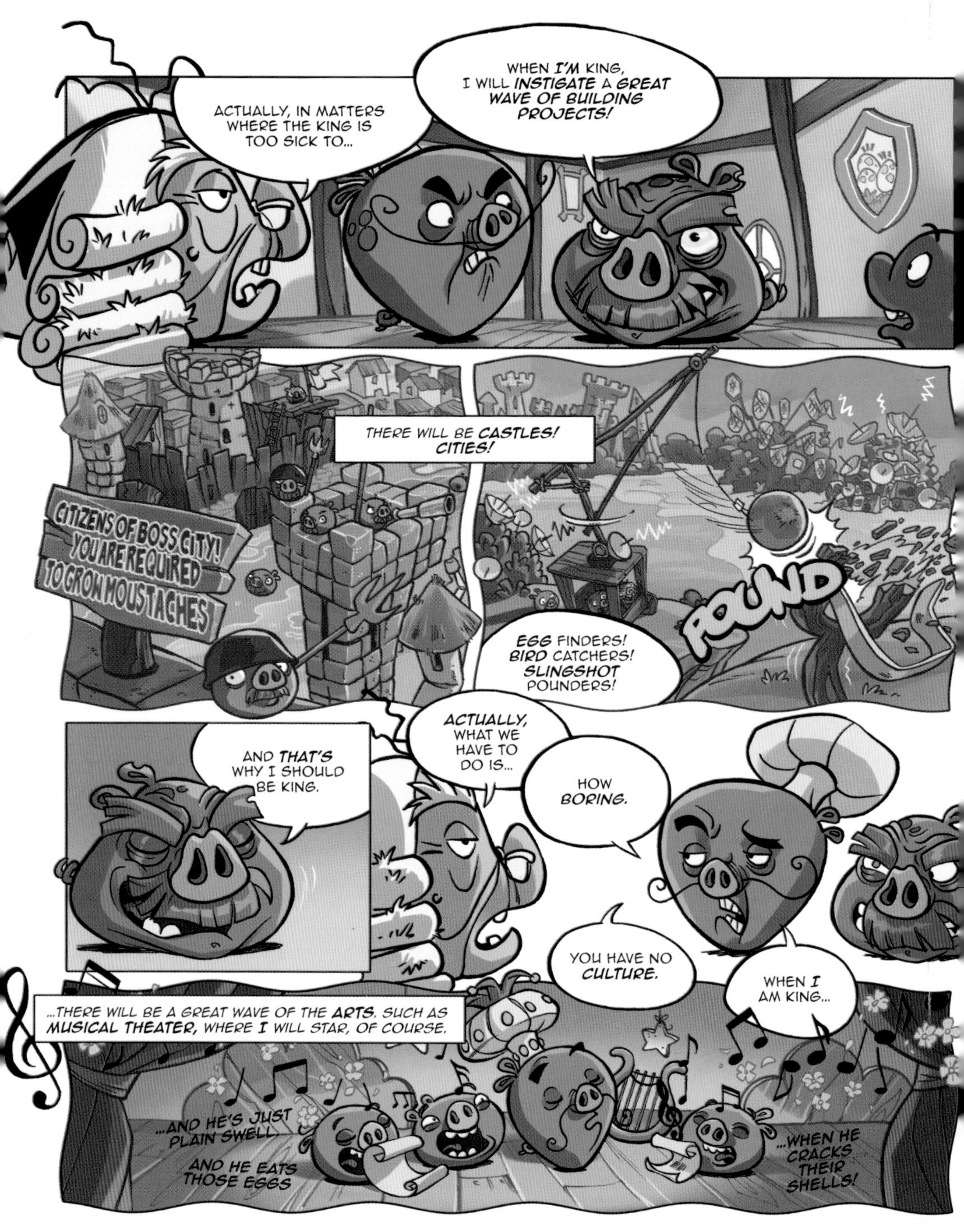
ACTUALLY, IN MATTERS WHERE THE KING IS TOO SICK TO...
WHEN I'M KING, I WILL INSTIGATE A GREAT WAVE OF BUILDING PROJECTS!
THERE WILL BE CASTLES! CITIES!
CITIZENS OF BOSS CITY! YOU ARE REQUIRED TO GROW MOUSTACHES
POUND
EGG FINDERS! BIRD CATCHERS! SLINGSHOT POUNDERS!
AND THAT'S WHY I SHOULD BE KING.
ACTUALLY, WHAT WE HAVE TO DO IS...
HOW BORING.
YOU HAVE NO CULTURE.
WHEN I AM KING...
...THERE WILL BE A GREAT WAVE OF THE ARTS. SUCH AS MUSICAL THEATER, WHERE I WILL STAR, OF COURSE.
...AND HE'S JUST PLAIN SWELL
AND HE EATS THOSE EGGS
...WHEN HE CRACKS THEIR SHELLS!

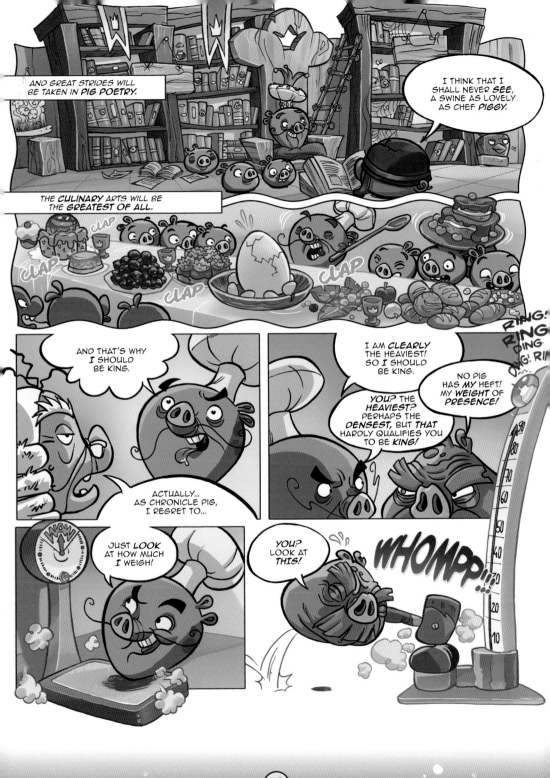

AND GREAT STRIDES WILL BE TAKEN IN *PIG POETRY.*

I THINK THAT I SHALL NEVER *SEE,* A SWINE AS LOVELY AS CHEF *PIGGY.*

THE *CULINARY ARTS* WILL BE THE *GREATEST OF ALL.*

CLAP

CLAP

CLAP

CLAP

AND THAT'S WHY *I* SHOULD BE KING.

I AM *CLEARLY* THE *HEAVIEST!* SO *I* SHOULD BE KING.

NO PIG HAS *MY* HEFT! MY *WEIGHT* OF *PRESENCE!*

YOU? THE *HEAVIEST?* PERHAPS THE *DENSEST,* BUT *THAT* HARDLY QUALIFIES YOU TO BE *KING!*

RING! RING! DING OMG! RIN

ACTUALLY... AS CHRONICLE PIG, I REGRET TO...

WOW

JUST *LOOK* AT HOW MUCH *I* WEIGH!

YOU? LOOK AT *THIS!*

WHOMPP!!!

90
80
70
60
50
40
30
20
10

NONE OF THAT, WHILE *ADMITTEDLY IMPRESSIVE*, MAKES ANY DIFFERENCE, BECAUSE...

I REGRET TO INFORM YOU THAT...

...WHEN THE KING IS UNABLE TO PERFORM HIS DUTIES, A *REPLACEMENT* IS TO BE CHOSEN BY...

LOTTERY

LOTTERY?

LOTTERY? THAT'S ABSURD.

ABSURD?!! THERE ARE RULES TO BE FOLLOWED! TRADITION TO BE HONORED! CUSTOMS AND RITUALS THAT HAVE MADE PIGS THE GREATEST OF ALL CREATURES!

WE'RE THE GREATEST?

I VOTED FOR *BUNNIES.*

SLAMMM!

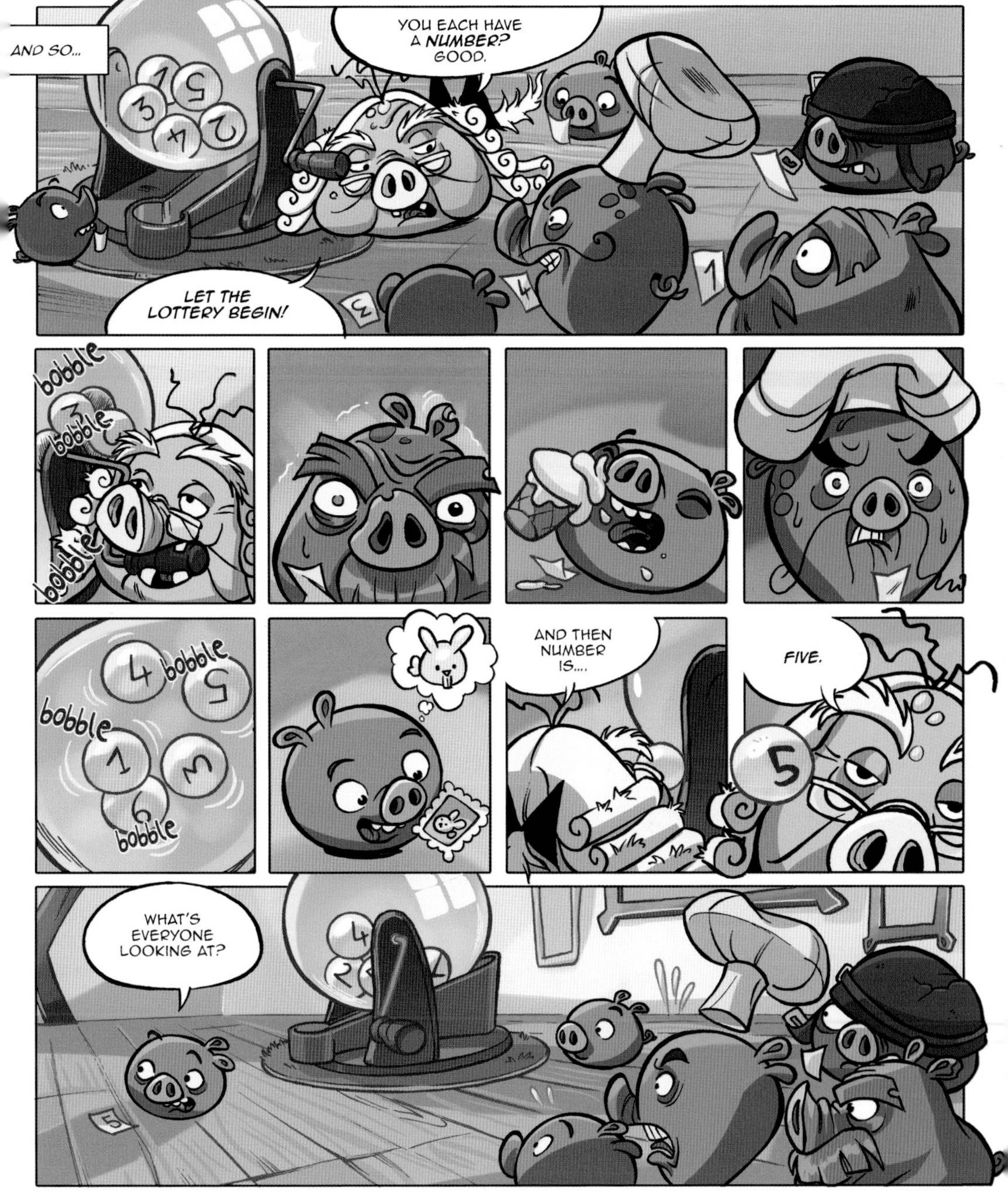
AND SO...
YOU EACH HAVE A NUMBER? GOOD.
LET THE LOTTERY BEGIN!
bobble
bobble
bobble
bobble
bobble
bobble
bobble
bobble
AND THEN NUMBER IS....
FIVE.
WHAT'S EVERYONE LOOKING AT?

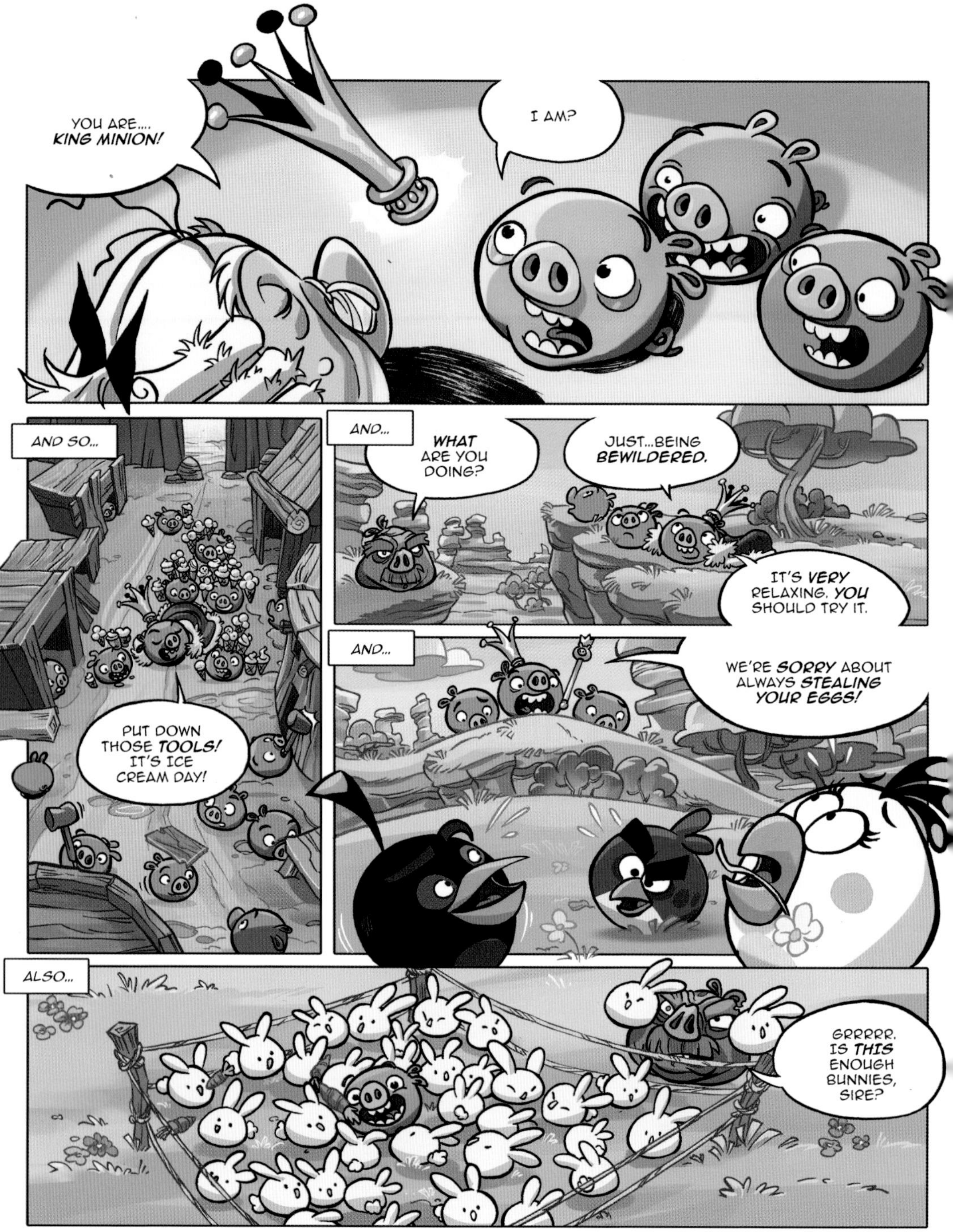
YOU ARE.... KING MINION!
I AM?
AND SO...
PUT DOWN THOSE TOOLS! IT'S ICE CREAM DAY!
AND...
WHAT ARE YOU DOING?
JUST...BEING BEWILDERED.
IT'S VERY RELAXING. YOU SHOULD TRY IT.
AND...
WE'RE SORRY ABOUT ALWAYS STEALING YOUR EGGS!
ALSO...
GRRRRR. IS THIS ENOUGH BUNNIES, SIRE?

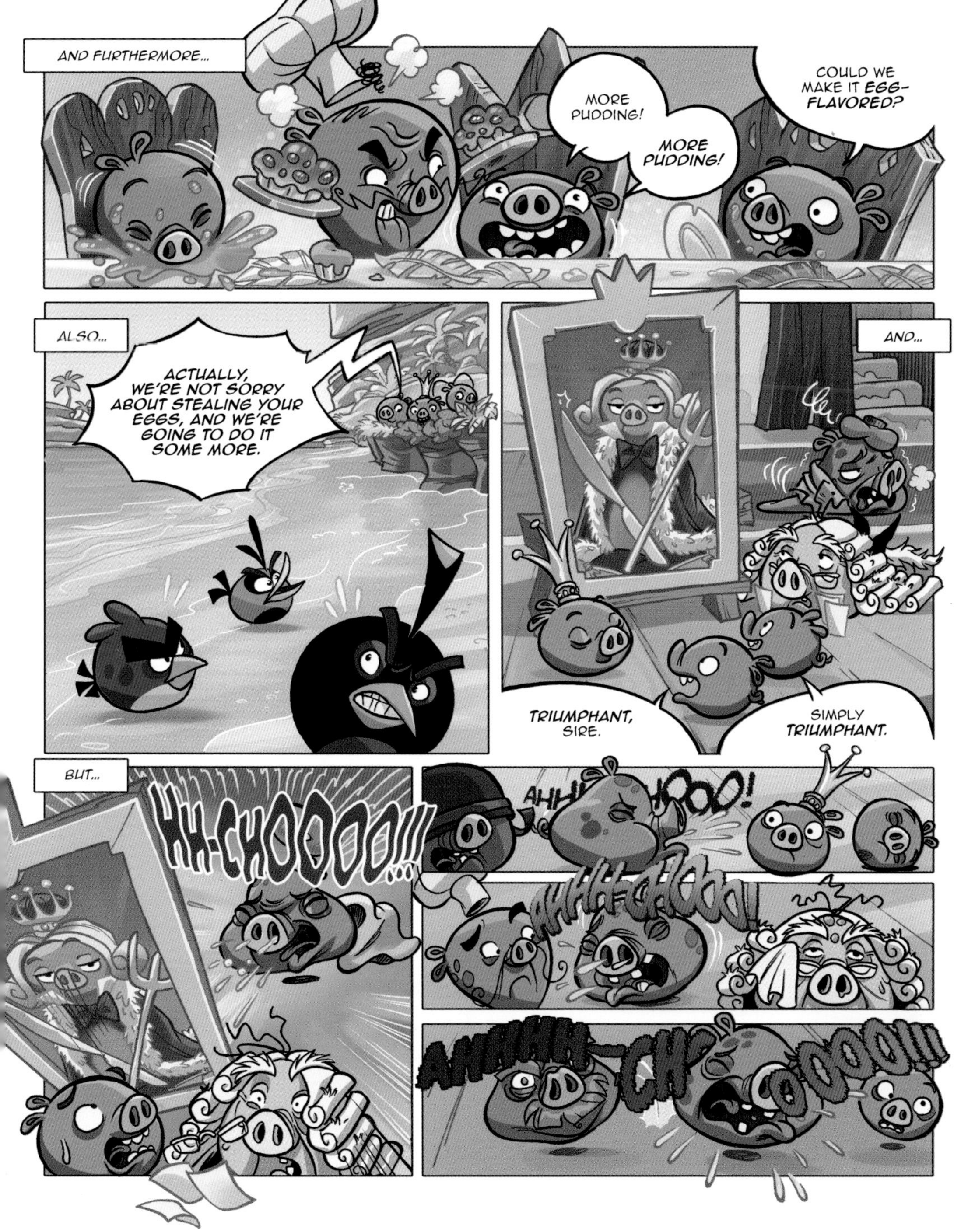
AND FURTHERMORE...
MORE PUDDING!
MORE PUDDING!
COULD WE MAKE IT EGG-FLAVORED?
ALSO...
ACTUALLY, WE'RE NOT SORRY ABOUT STEALING YOUR EGGS, AND WE'RE GOING TO DO IT SOME MORE.
AND...
TRIUMPHANT, SIRE.
SIMPLY TRIUMPHANT.
BUT...
HH-CHOOOOO!!!
AHHH-CHOOO!
AHHH-CHOOOO!
AHHHH-CHOOOO!!!

AHHH-CHOOo
AH-CHOOO!!
SNIRRFF
AHHHH
AAHHHH-
AHH-CHIIII
CHOOOO!
HMMM, WELL, SINCE WE **ALL** HAVE THE PIGGY SNIFFLES, IT MAKES NO DIFFERENCE. I PRONOUNCE YOU... ***CHUFF CHUFF...*** ***KING*** ONCE MORE!
THIS WHOLE EPISODE... *SNIFF SNUFFLE...* HAS BEEN INTOLERABLE. I HAVE ONLY ***ONE*** COMMENT.
YES, MY KING?
AHHHHHH
THE END

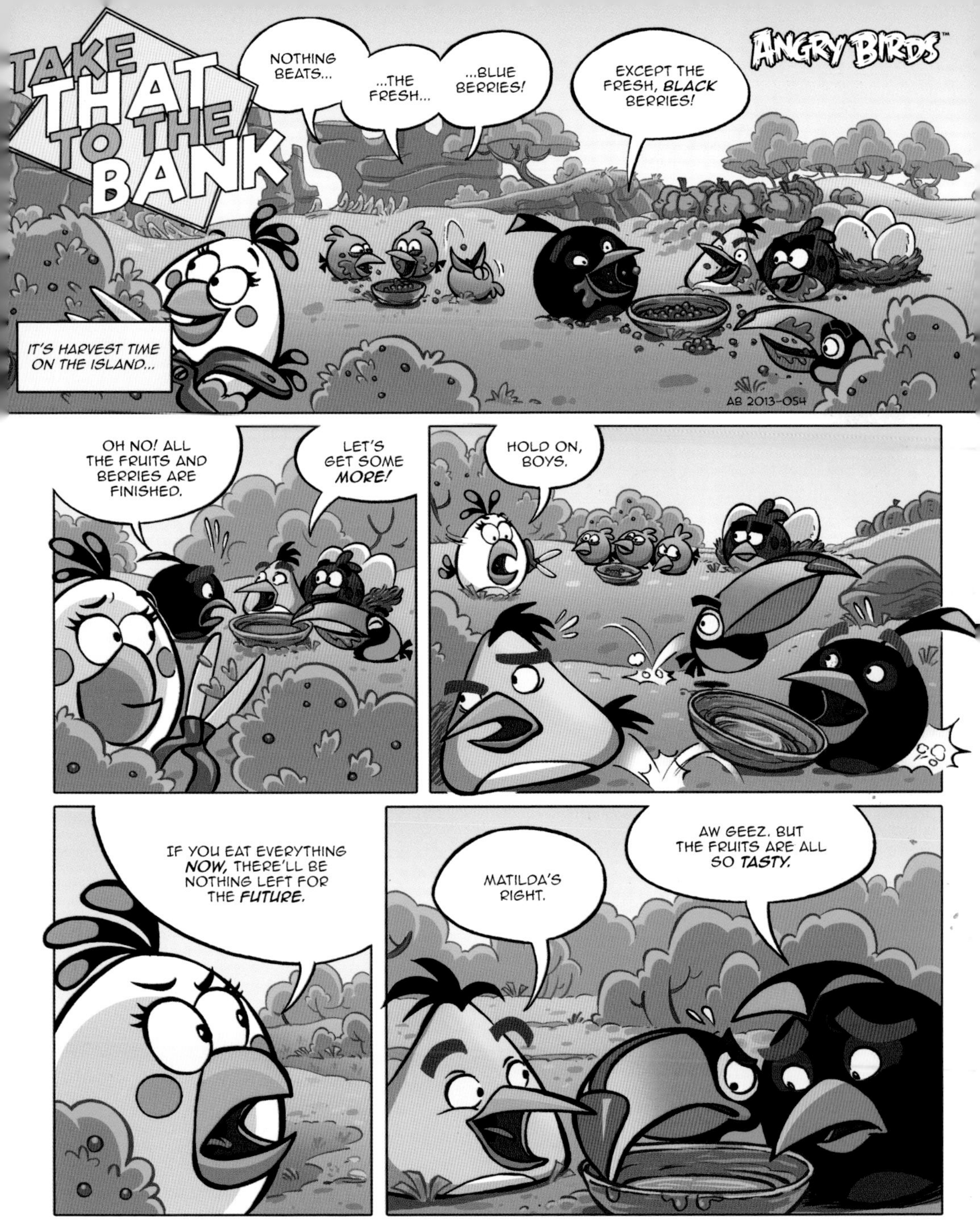
TAKE THAT TO THE BANK
ANGRY BIRDS™
NOTHING BEATS...
...THE FRESH...
...BLUE BERRIES!
EXCEPT THE FRESH, BLACK BERRIES!
IT'S HARVEST TIME ON THE ISLAND...
AB 2013-054
OH NO! ALL THE FRUITS AND BERRIES ARE FINISHED.
LET'S GET SOME MORE!
HOLD ON, BOYS.
IF YOU EAT EVERYTHING NOW, THERE'LL BE NOTHING LEFT FOR THE FUTURE.
MATILDA'S RIGHT.
AW GEEZ. BUT THE FRUITS ARE ALL SO TASTY.

WRITTEN BY: JANNE TORISEVA • ART BY: AUDREY BUSSI • COLORS BY: DIGIKORE • LETTERS BY: PISARA OY

HEY, WHAT ON EARTH ARE YOU DOING, MATILDA?!
WHY ARE YOU...
...DESTROYING OUR FAVORITE BUSH?!
I'M NOT DESTROYING THE BUSH. ACTUALLY, I'M DOING THE *OPPOSITE...*
IT CAN'T GROW ANY BIGGER IN THAT PLACE. THAT'S WHY I'M TAKING CUTTINGS FROM IT AND PLANTING THEM IN ANOTHER AREA TO GROW.
IF YOU GIVE THEM SOME TIME TO GROW, YOU'LL EVENTUALLY GET EVEN MORE BERRIES.
HOW GREAT IS THAT?!
BUT WHY HAVE YOU SPREAD THE CUTTINGS *ALL AROUND* THE GARDEN?

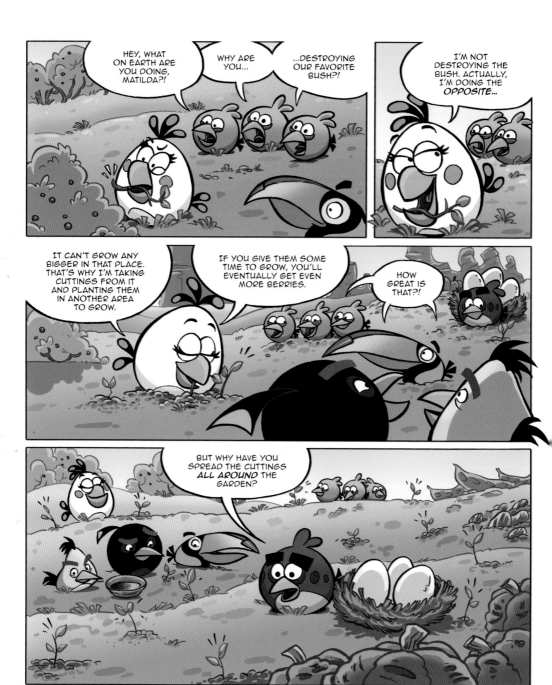

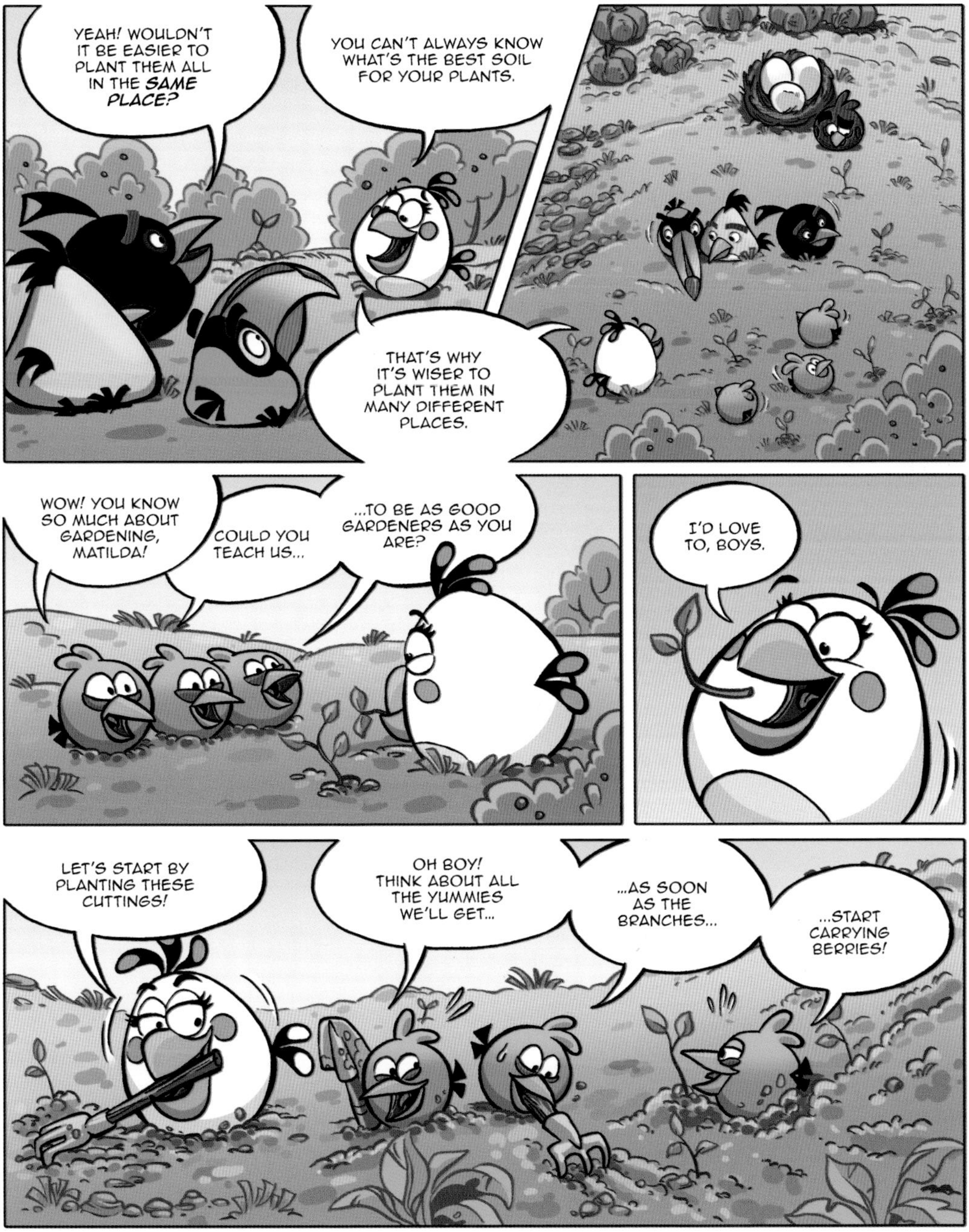
YEAH! WOULDN'T IT BE EASIER TO PLANT THEM ALL IN THE *SAME PLACE?*
YOU CAN'T ALWAYS KNOW WHAT'S THE BEST SOIL FOR YOUR PLANTS.
THAT'S WHY IT'S WISER TO PLANT THEM IN MANY DIFFERENT PLACES.
WOW! YOU KNOW SO MUCH ABOUT GARDENING, MATILDA!
COULD YOU TEACH US...
...TO BE AS GOOD GARDENERS AS YOU ARE?
I'D LOVE TO, BOYS.
LET'S START BY PLANTING THESE CUTTINGS!
OH BOY! THINK ABOUT ALL THE YUMMIES WE'LL GET...
...AS SOON AS THE BRANCHES...
...START CARRYING BERRIES!

AT THE SAME TIME:
AAAH! THESE FRUITS'N BERRIES MUST BE SO TASTY!
THEY SURE MUST BE!
TOO BAD THAT WE CAN'T EAT ANY OF THEM.
WELL, THINK ABOUT THE BRIGHT SIDE OF IT.
AS LONG AS THE KING THINKS OF THE HARVEST INSTEAD OF THE EGGS...
WE WON'T GET BEATEN BY THE BIRDS!

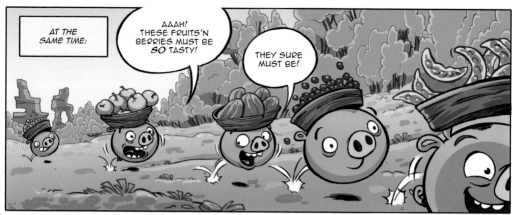

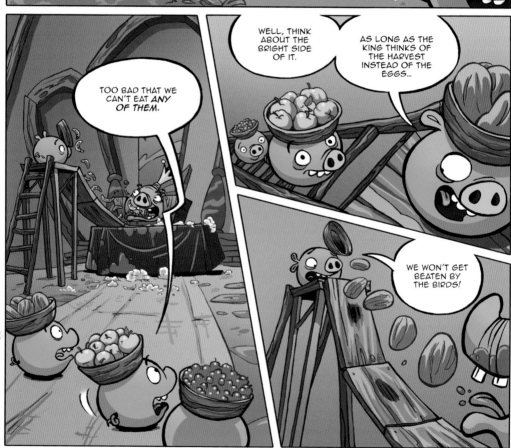

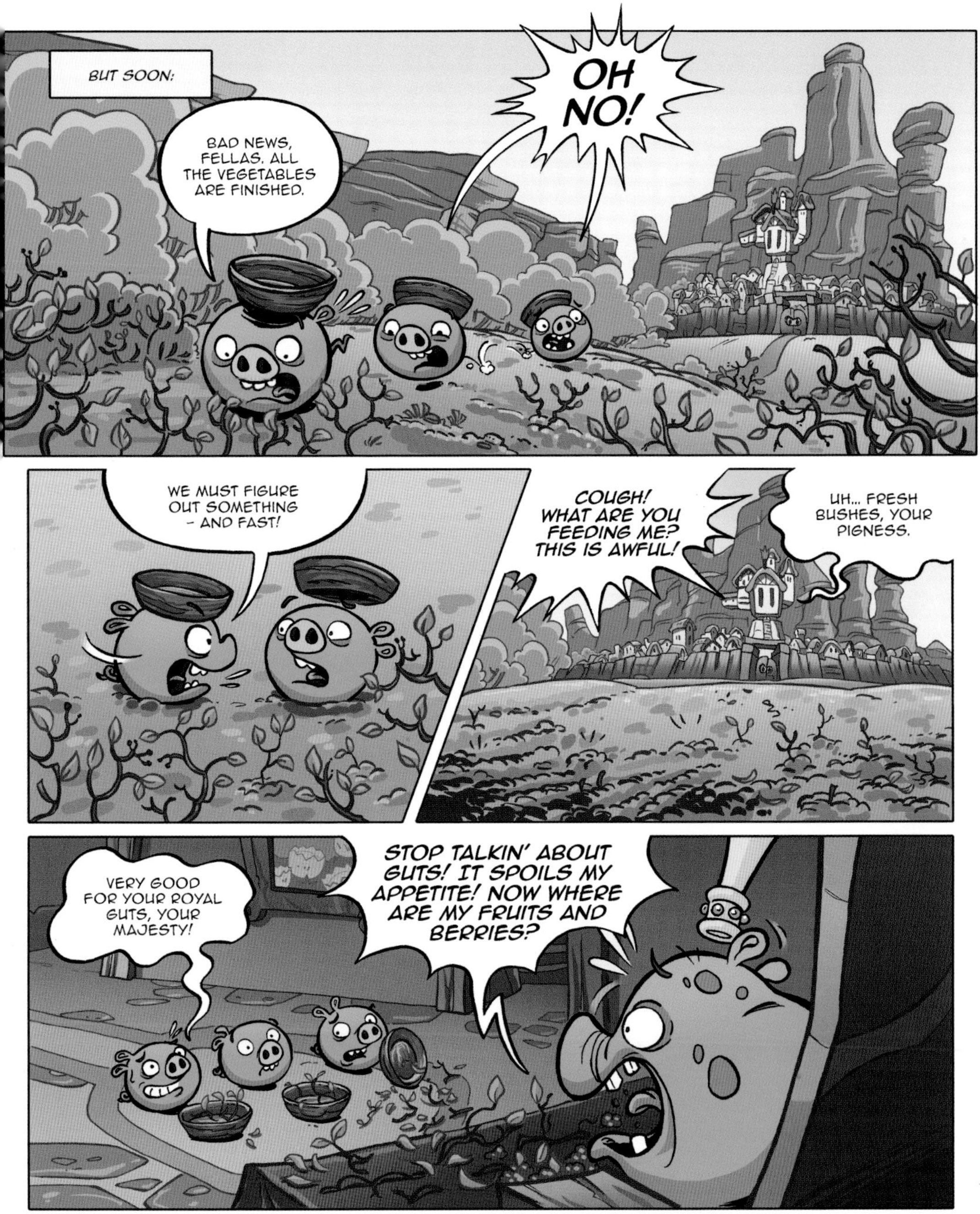
BUT SOON:
BAD NEWS, FELLAS. ALL THE VEGETABLES ARE FINISHED.
OH NO!
WE MUST FIGURE OUT SOMETHING - AND FAST!
COUGH! WHAT ARE YOU FEEDING ME? THIS IS AWFUL!
UH... FRESH BUSHES, YOUR PIGNESS.
VERY GOOD FOR YOUR ROYAL GUTS, YOUR MAJESTY!
STOP TALKIN' ABOUT GUTS! IT SPOILS MY APPETITE! NOW WHERE ARE MY FRUITS AND BERRIES?

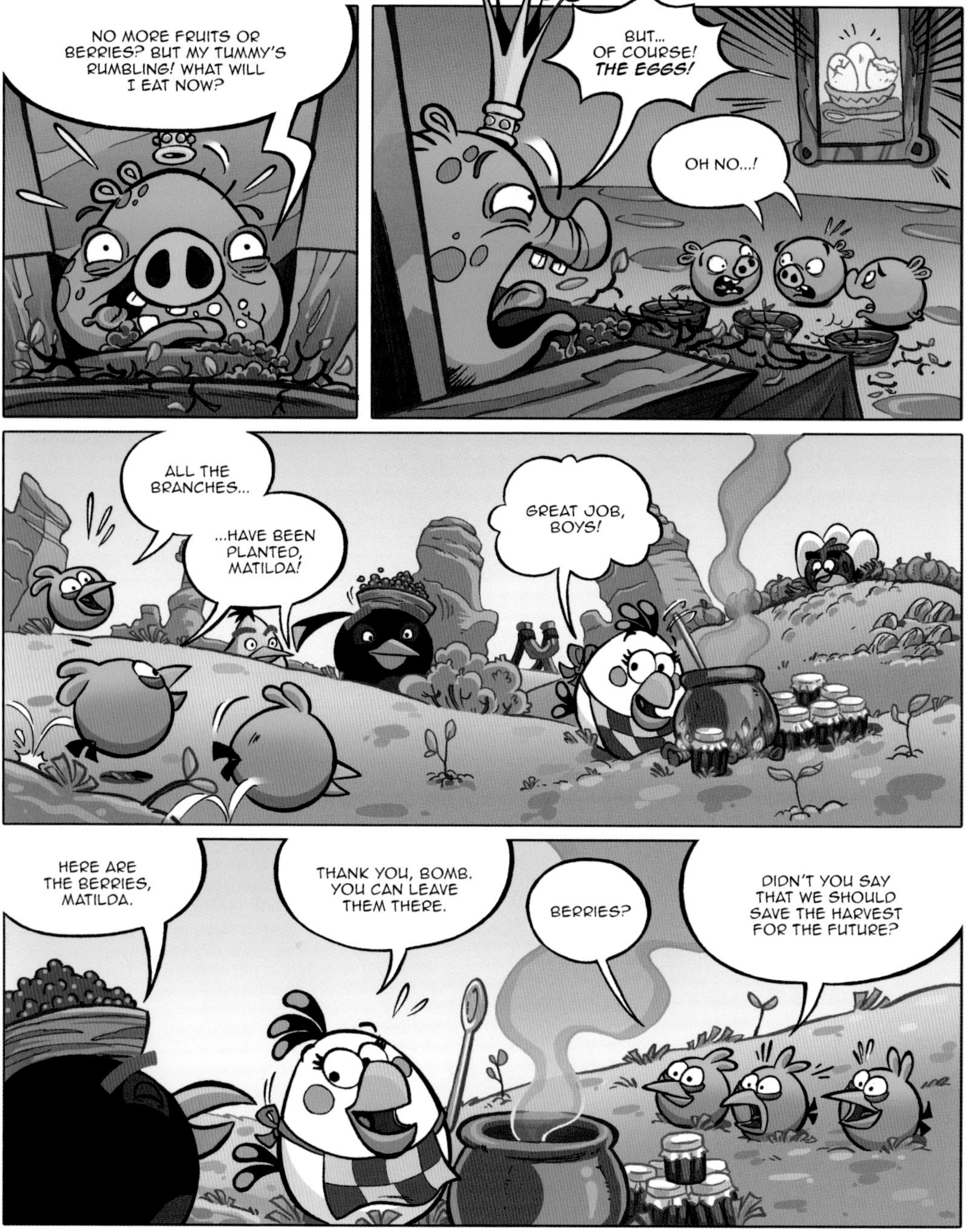
NO MORE FRUITS OR BERRIES? BUT MY TUMMY'S RUMBLING! WHAT WILL I EAT NOW?
BUT... OF COURSE! ***THE EGGS!***
OH NO...!
ALL THE BRANCHES...
...HAVE BEEN PLANTED, MATILDA!
GREAT JOB, BOYS!
HERE ARE THE BERRIES, MATILDA.
THANK YOU, BOMB. YOU CAN LEAVE THEM THERE.
BERRIES?
DIDN'T YOU SAY THAT WE SHOULD SAVE THE HARVEST FOR THE FUTURE?

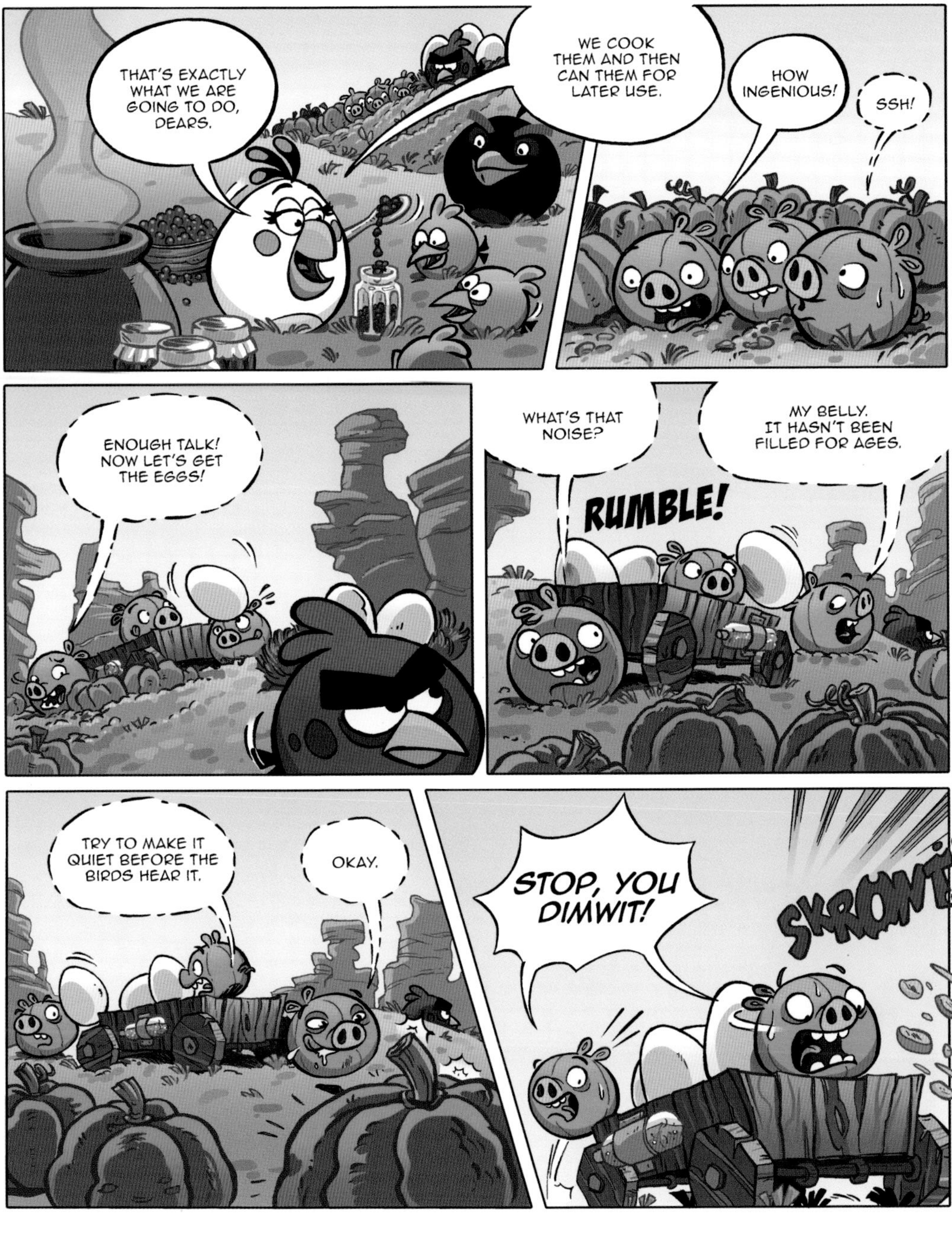
THAT'S EXACTLY WHAT WE ARE GOING TO DO, DEARS.
WE COOK THEM AND THEN CAN THEM FOR LATER USE.
HOW INGENIOUS!
SSH!
ENOUGH TALK! NOW LET'S GET THE EGGS!
WHAT'S THAT NOISE?
MY BELLY. IT HASN'T BEEN FILLED FOR AGES.
RUMBLE!
TRY TO MAKE IT QUIET BEFORE THE BIRDS HEAR IT.
OKAY.
STOP, YOU DIMWIT!
SKRONT!

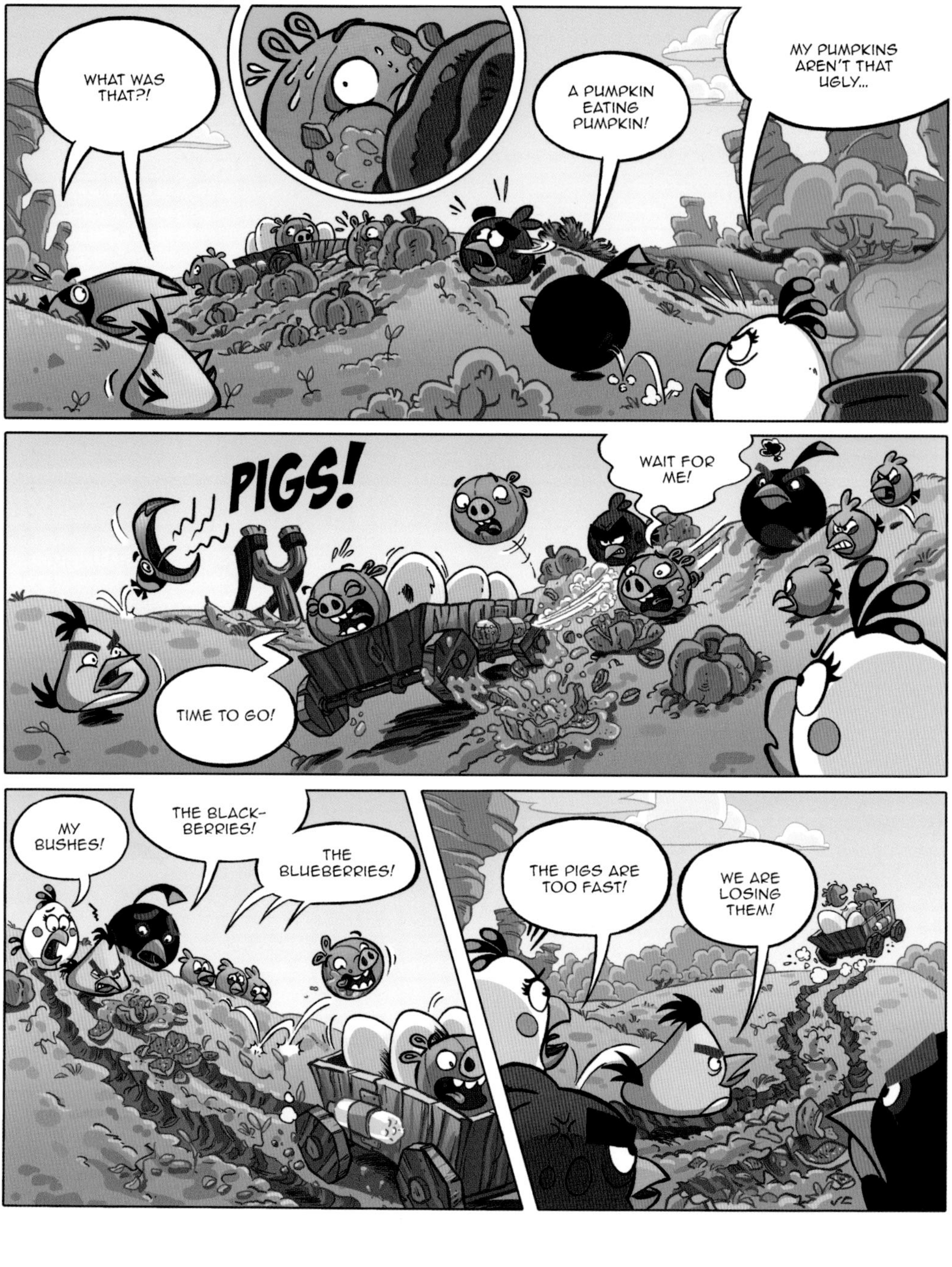
WHAT WAS THAT?!
A PUMPKIN EATING PUMPKIN!
MY PUMPKINS AREN'T THAT UGLY...
PIGS!
WAIT FOR ME!
TIME TO GO!
MY BUSHES!
THE BLACK-BERRIES!
THE BLUEBERRIES!
THE PIGS ARE TOO FAST!
WE ARE LOSING THEM!

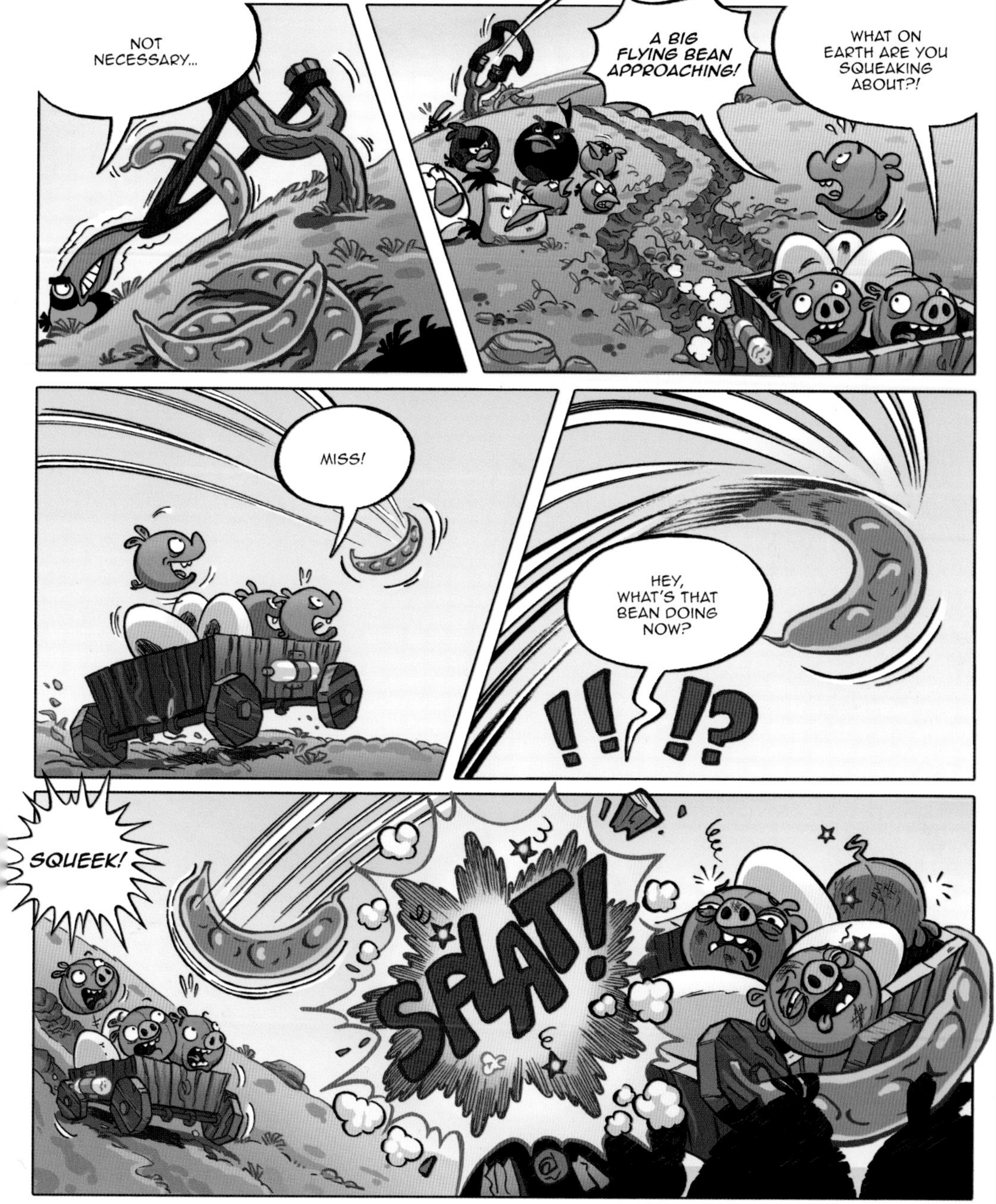
NOT NECESSARY...
A BIG FLYING BEAN APPROACHING!
WHAT ON EARTH ARE YOU SQUEAKING ABOUT?!
MISS!
HEY, WHAT'S THAT BEAN DOING NOW?
!!!?
SQUEEK!
SPLAT!

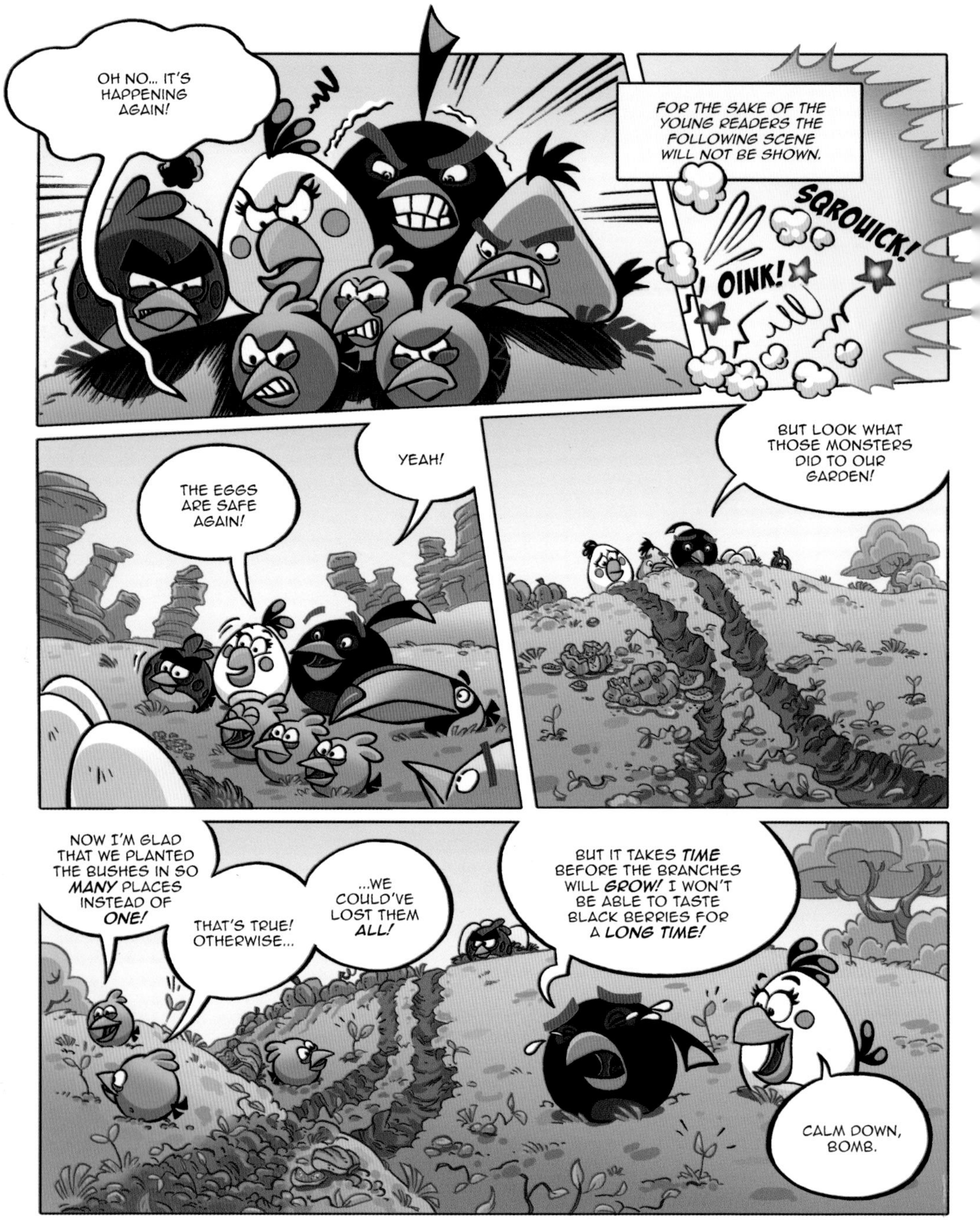

OH NO... IT'S HAPPENING AGAIN!
FOR THE SAKE OF THE YOUNG READERS THE FOLLOWING SCENE WILL NOT BE SHOWN.
SQROUICK!
OINK!
THE EGGS ARE SAFE AGAIN!
YEAH!
BUT LOOK WHAT THOSE MONSTERS DID TO OUR GARDEN!
NOW I'M GLAD THAT WE PLANTED THE BUSHES IN SO MANY PLACES INSTEAD OF ONE!
THAT'S TRUE! OTHERWISE...
...WE COULD'VE LOST THEM ALL!
BUT IT TAKES TIME BEFORE THE BRANCHES WILL GROW! I WON'T BE ABLE TO TASTE BLACK BERRIES FOR A LONG TIME!
CALM DOWN, BOMB.

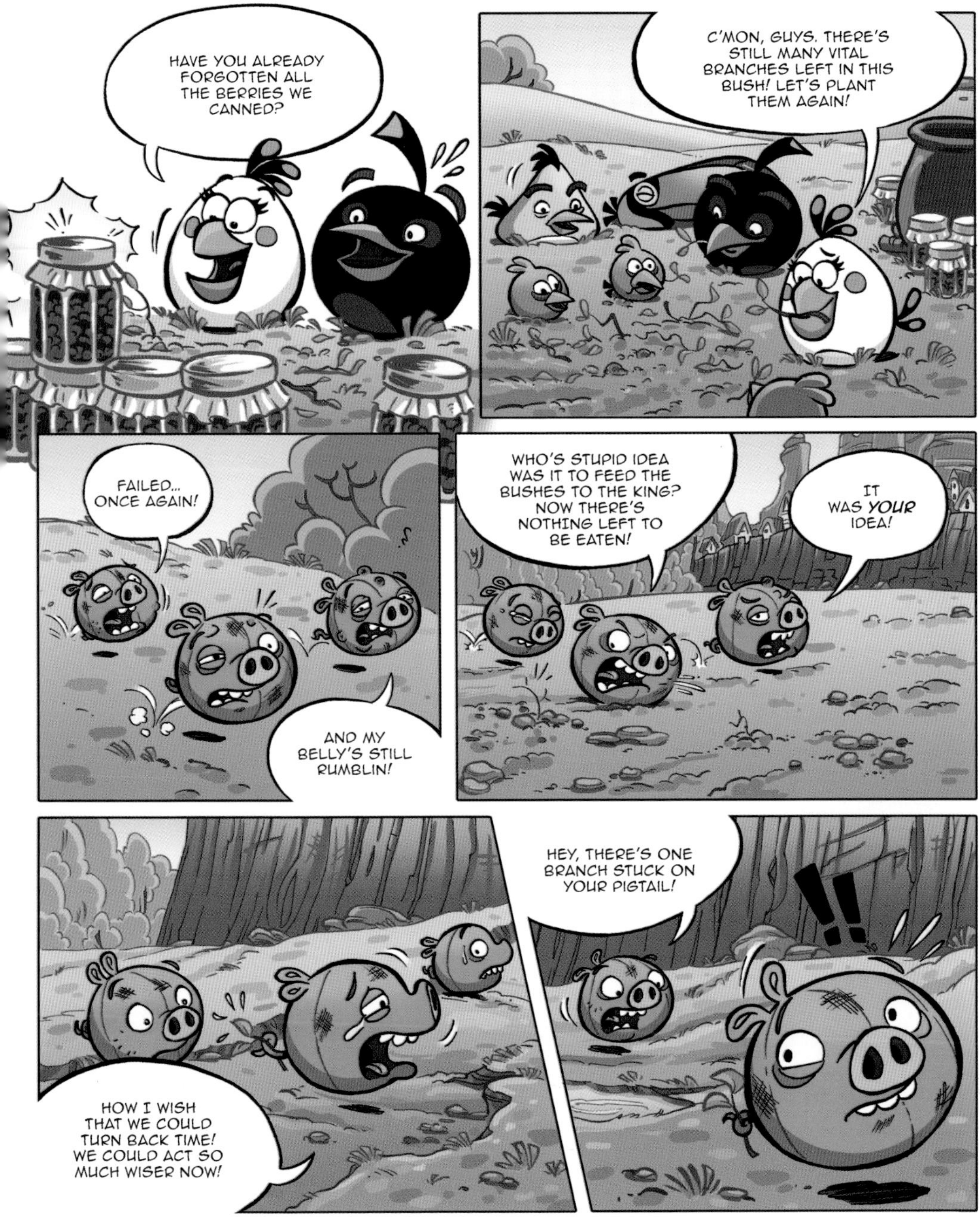
HAVE YOU ALREADY FORGOTTEN ALL THE BERRIES WE CANNED?
C'MON, GUYS. THERE'S STILL MANY VITAL BRANCHES LEFT IN THIS BUSH! LET'S PLANT THEM AGAIN!
FAILED... ONCE AGAIN!
AND MY BELLY'S STILL RUMBLIN!
WHO'S STUPID IDEA WAS IT TO FEED THE BUSHES TO THE KING? NOW THERE'S NOTHING LEFT TO BE EATEN!
IT WAS *YOUR* IDEA!
HOW I WISH THAT WE COULD TURN BACK TIME! WE COULD ACT SO MUCH WISER NOW!
HEY, THERE'S ONE BRANCH STUCK ON YOUR PIGTAIL!
!!

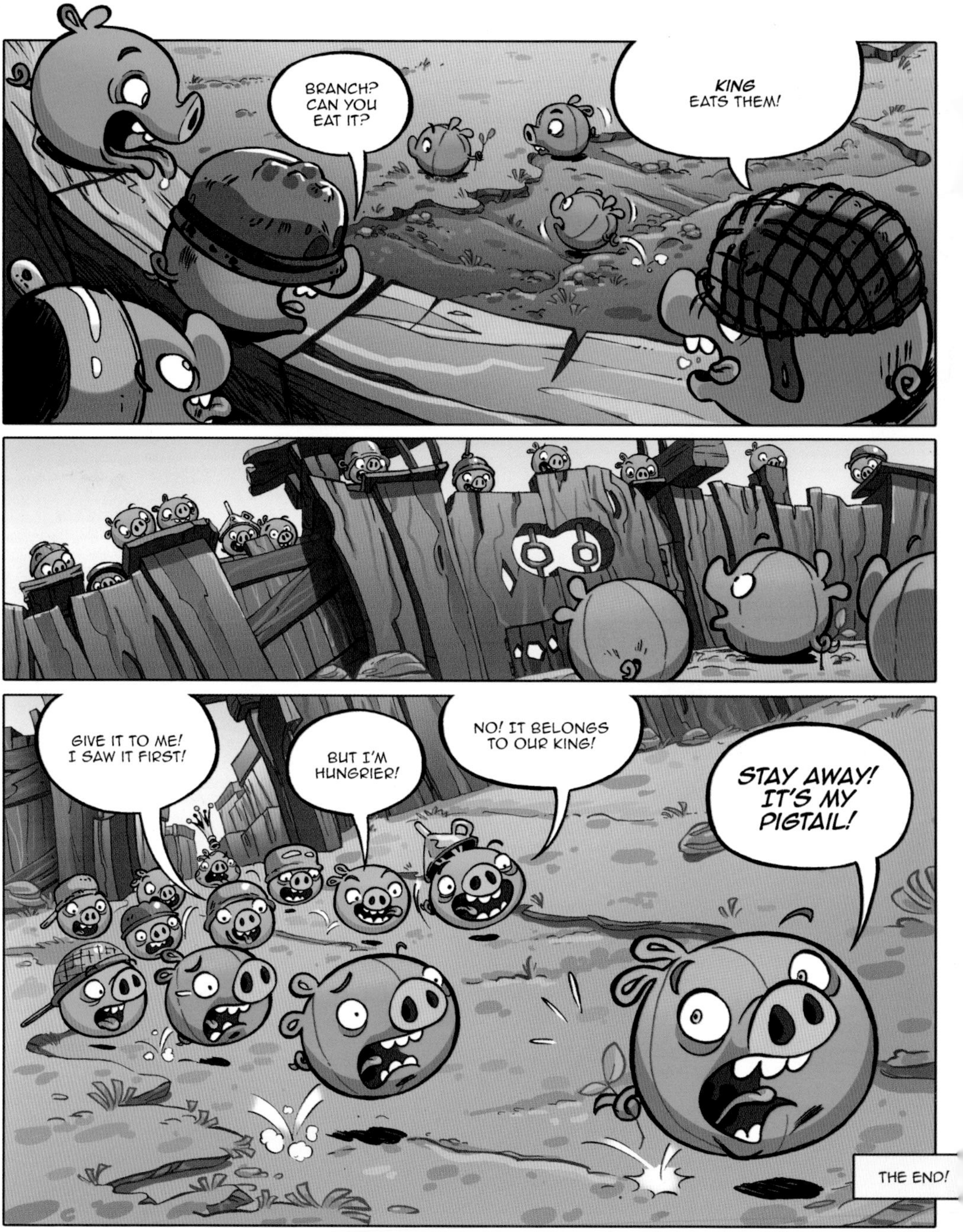
BRANCH? CAN YOU EAT IT?
KING EATS THEM!
GIVE IT TO ME! I SAW IT FIRST!
BUT I'M HUNGRIER!
NO! IT BELONGS TO OUR KING!
STAY AWAY! IT'S MY PIGTAIL!
THE END!

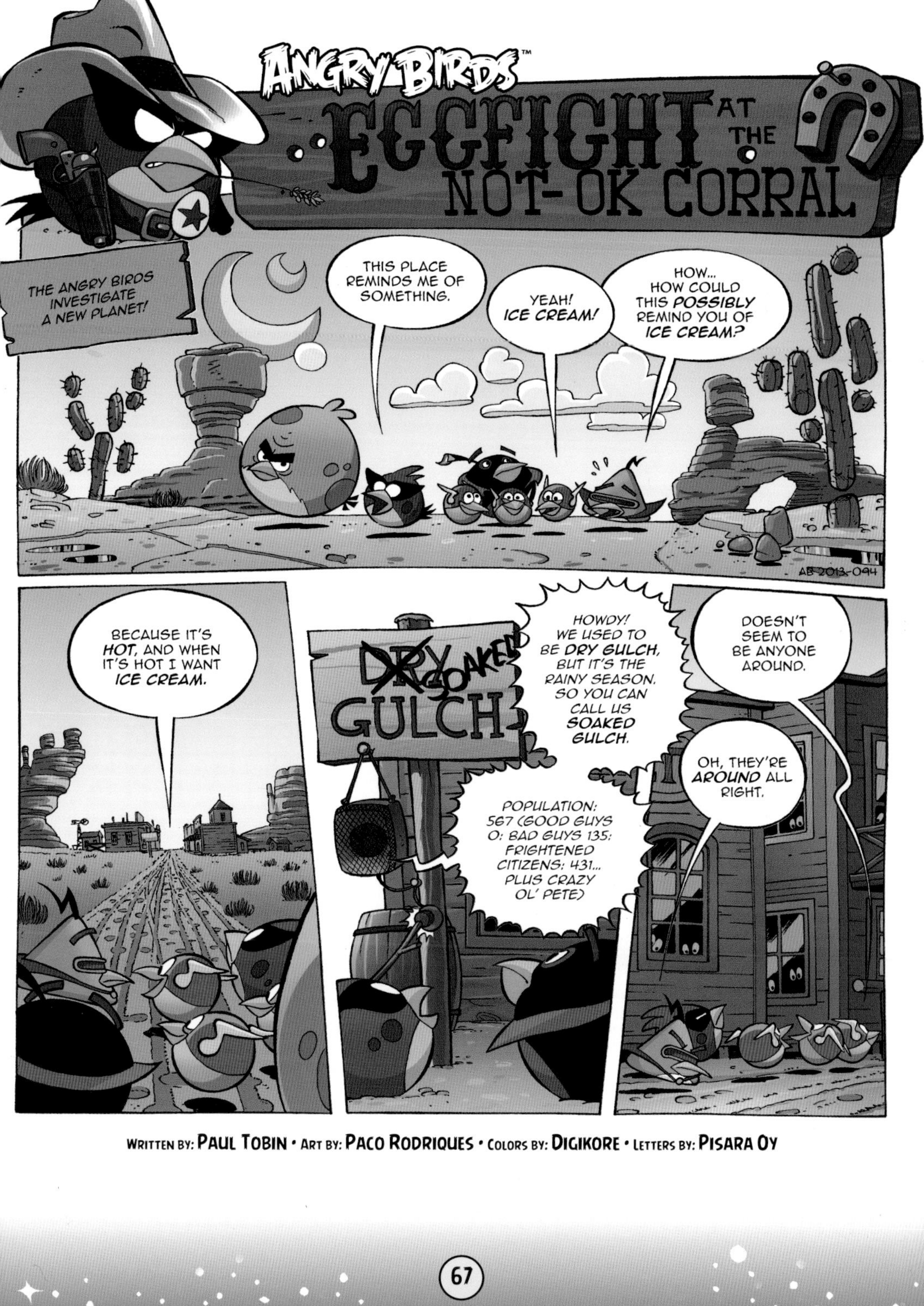
ANGRY BIRDS™
EGGFIGHT AT THE NOT-OK CORRAL
THE ANGRY BIRDS INVESTIGATE A NEW PLANET!
THIS PLACE REMINDS ME OF SOMETHING.
YEAH! *ICE CREAM!*
HOW... HOW COULD THIS *POSSIBLY* REMIND YOU OF *ICE CREAM?*
AB 2013-094
BECAUSE IT'S *HOT*, AND WHEN IT'S HOT I WANT *ICE CREAM.*
DRY SOAKED GULCH
HOWDY! WE USED TO BE **DRY GULCH**, BUT IT'S THE RAINY SEASON. SO YOU CAN CALL US **SOAKED GULCH**.
POPULATION: 567 (GOOD GUYS 0: BAD GUYS 135: FRIGHTENED CITIZENS: 431... PLUS CRAZY OL' PETE)
DOESN'T SEEM TO BE ANYONE AROUND.
OH, THEY'RE *AROUND* ALL RIGHT.

WRITTEN BY: **PAUL TOBIN** • ART BY: **PACO RODRIQUES** • COLORS BY: **DIGIKORE** • LETTERS BY: **PISARA OY**

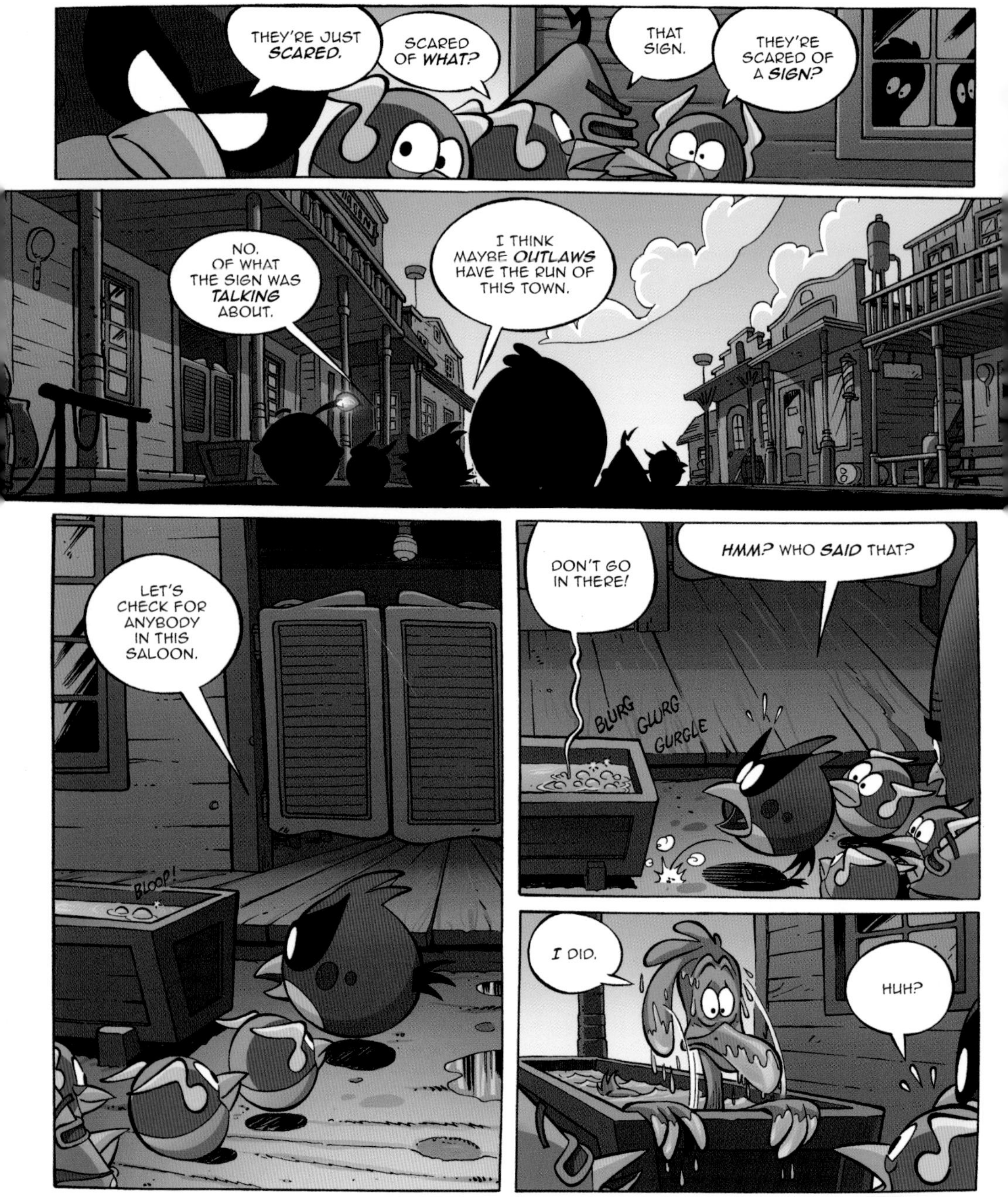

THEY'RE JUST SCARED.
SCARED OF WHAT?
THAT SIGN.
THEY'RE SCARED OF A SIGN?
NO. OF WHAT THE SIGN WAS TALKING ABOUT.
I THINK MAYBE OUTLAWS HAVE THE RUN OF THIS TOWN.
LET'S CHECK FOR ANYBODY IN THIS SALOON.
BLOOP!
DON'T GO IN THERE!
HMM? WHO SAID THAT?
BLURG
GLURG
GURGLE
I DID.
HUH?

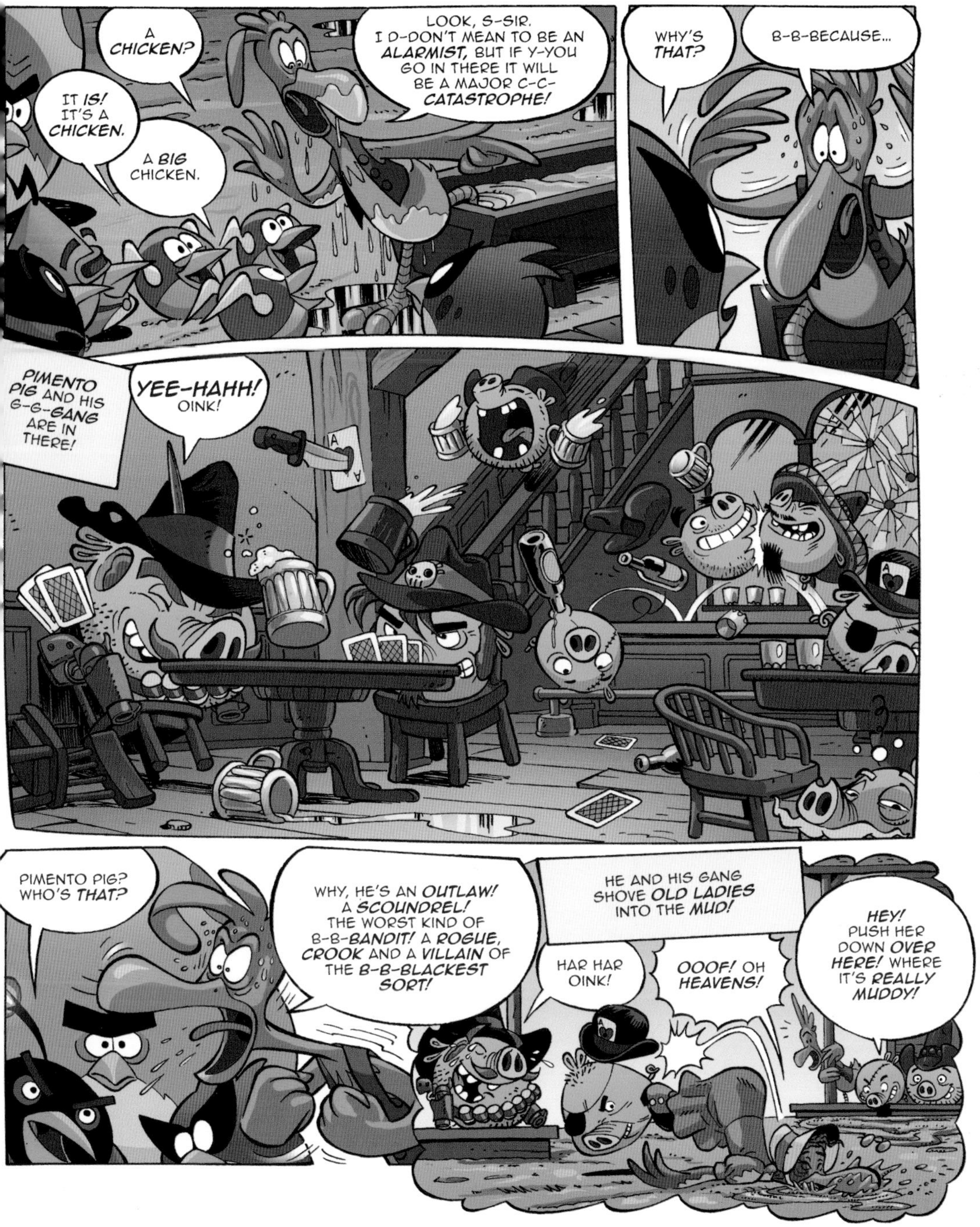
A CHICKEN?
IT IS! IT'S A CHICKEN.
A BIG CHICKEN.
LOOK, S-SIR. I D-DON'T MEAN TO BE AN ALARMIST, BUT IF Y-YOU GO IN THERE IT WILL BE A MAJOR C-C-CATASTROPHE!
WHY'S THAT?
B-B-BECAUSE...
PIMENTO PIG AND HIS G-G-GANG ARE IN THERE!
YEE-HAHH! OINK!
PIMENTO PIG? WHO'S THAT?
WHY, HE'S AN OUTLAW! A SCOUNDREL! THE WORST KIND OF B-B-BANDIT! A ROGUE, CROOK AND A VILLAIN OF THE B-B-BLACKEST SORT!
HE AND HIS GANG SHOVE OLD LADIES INTO THE MUD!
HAR HAR OINK!
OOOF! OH HEAVENS!
HEY! PUSH HER DOWN OVER HERE! WHERE IT'S REALLY MUDDY!

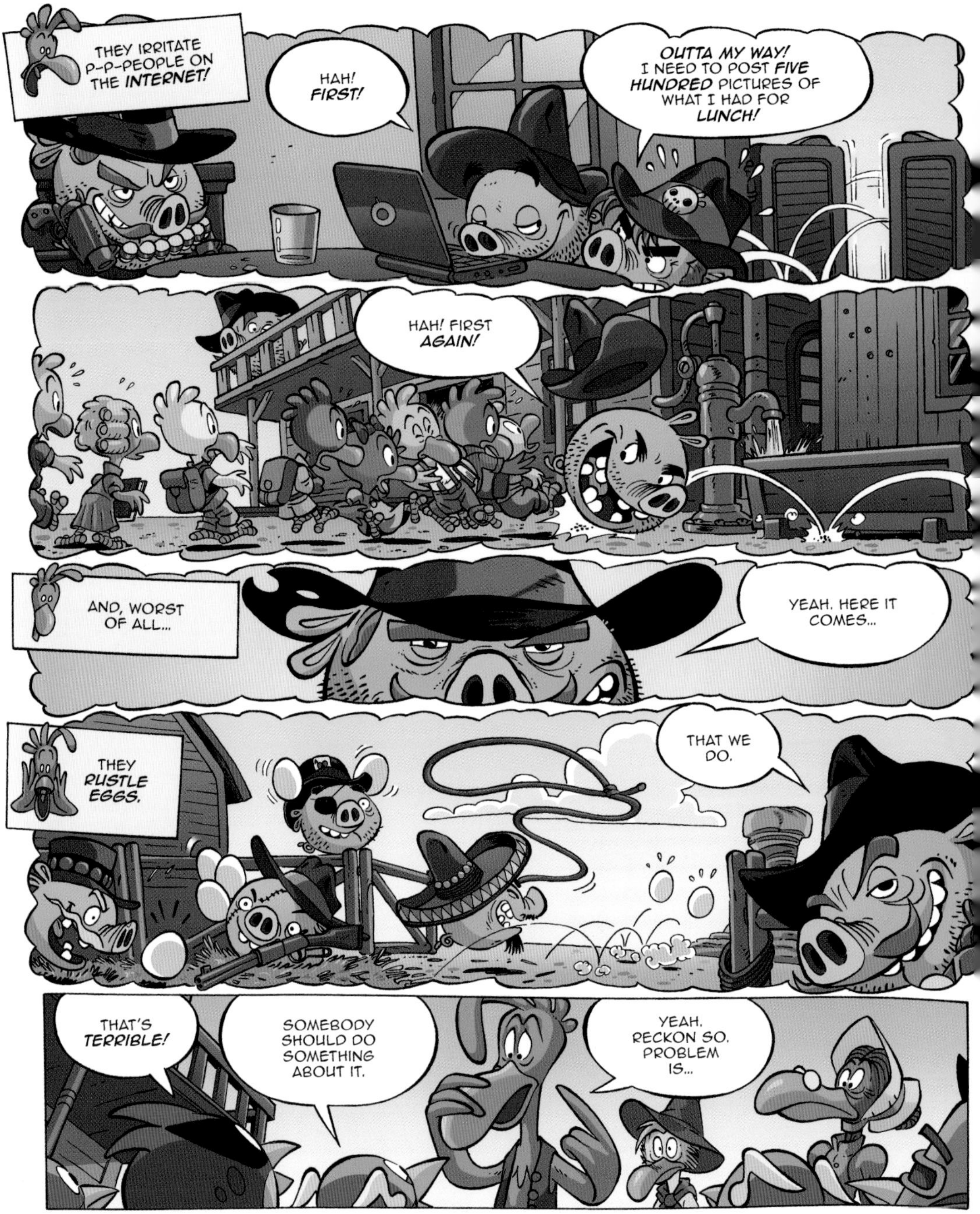
THEY IRRITATE P-P-PEOPLE ON THE INTERNET!
HAH! FIRST!
OUTTA MY WAY! I NEED TO POST FIVE HUNDRED PICTURES OF WHAT I HAD FOR LUNCH!
HAH! FIRST AGAIN!
AND, WORST OF ALL...
YEAH. HERE IT COMES...
THEY RUSTLE EGGS.
THAT WE DO.
THAT'S TERRIBLE!
SOMEBODY SHOULD DO SOMETHING ABOUT IT.
YEAH. RECKON SO. PROBLEM IS...

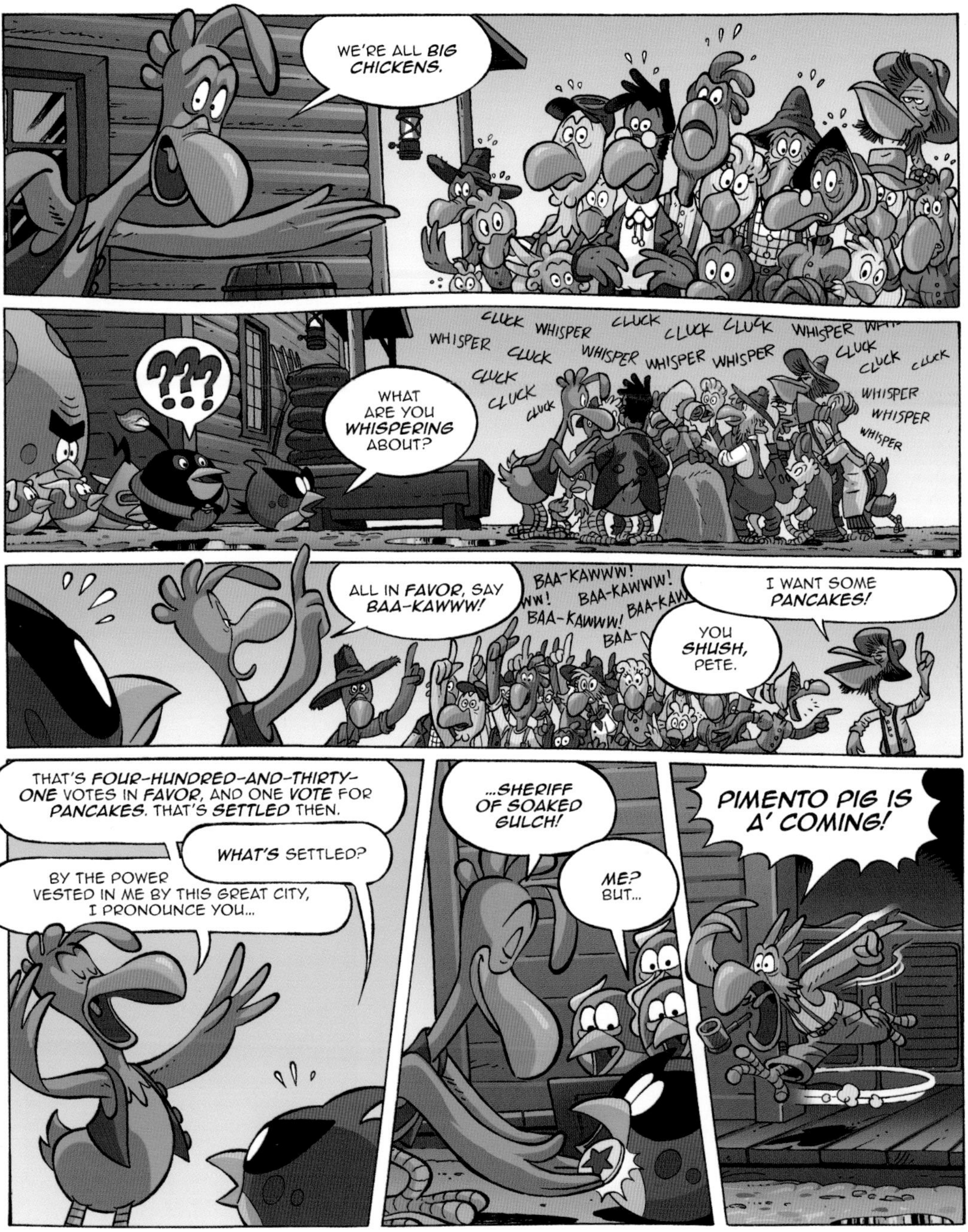
WE'RE ALL BIG CHICKENS.
CLUCK WHISPER CLUCK CLUCK CLUCK WHISPER WHISPER CLUCK WHISPER WHISPER WHISPER CLUCK CLUCK CLUCK CLUCK CLUCK WHISPER WHISPER WHISPER
???
WHAT ARE YOU WHISPERING ABOUT?
ALL IN FAVOR, SAY BAA-KAWWW!
BAA-KAWWW! BAA-KAWWW! BAA-KAWWW! BAA-KAWWW!
I WANT SOME PANCAKES!
YOU SHUSH, PETE.
THAT'S FOUR-HUNDRED-AND-THIRTY-ONE VOTES IN FAVOR, AND ONE VOTE FOR PANCAKES. THAT'S SETTLED THEN.
WHAT'S SETTLED?
BY THE POWER VESTED IN ME BY THIS GREAT CITY, I PRONOUNCE YOU...
...SHERIFF OF SOAKED GULCH!
ME? BUT...
PIMENTO PIG IS A' COMING!

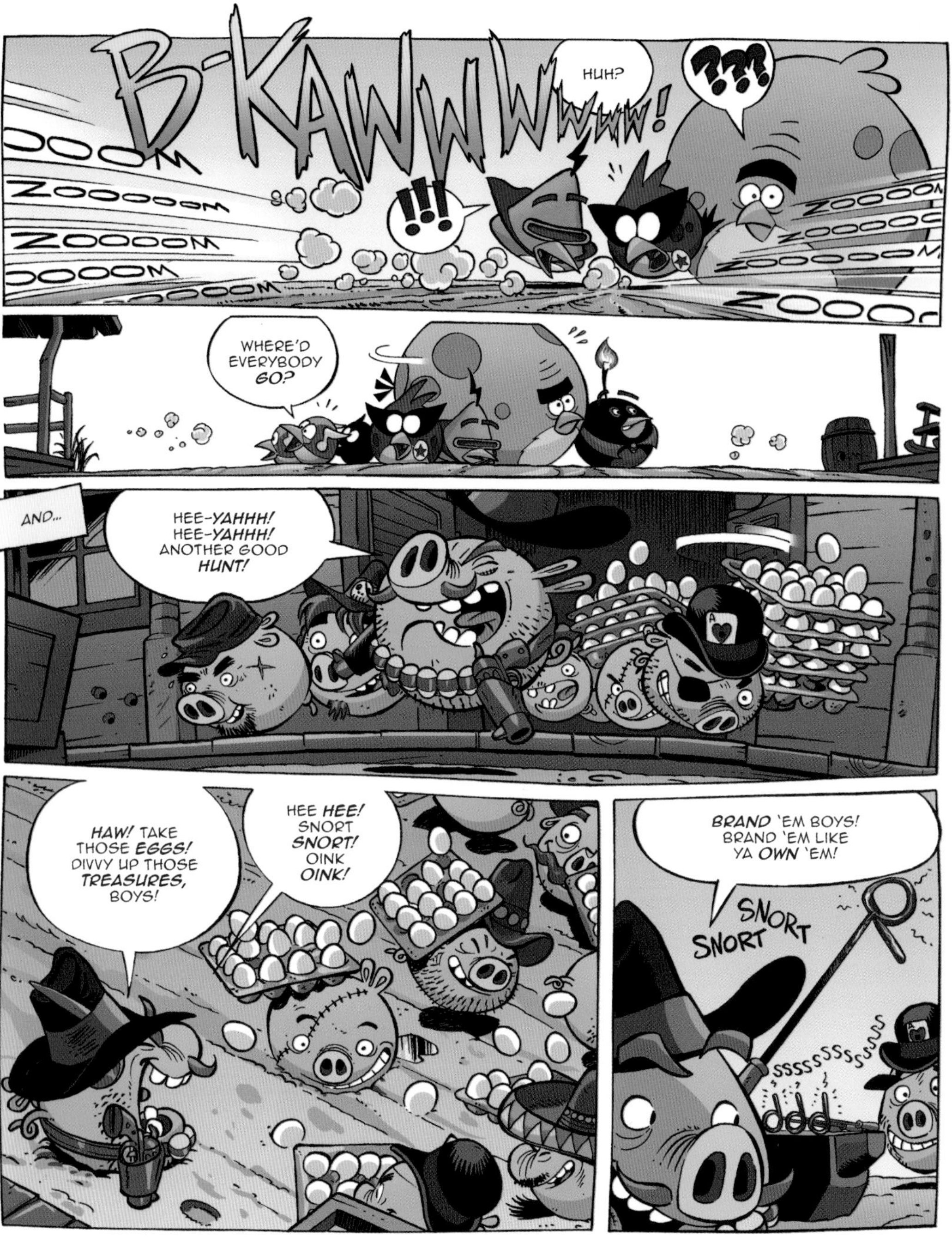
B-KAWWWwww!
HUH?
???
ZOOOOOOM
ZOOOOOM
OOOOM
ZOOOOOOM
ZOOOOOOOM
ZOOOO
!!!
WHERE'D EVERYBODY GO?
AND...
HEE-YAHHH! HEE-YAHHH! ANOTHER GOOD HUNT!
HAW! TAKE THOSE EGGS! DIVVY UP THOSE TREASURES, BOYS!
HEE HEE! SNORT SNORT! OINK OINK!
BRAND 'EM BOYS! BRAND 'EM LIKE YA OWN 'EM!
SNORT SNORT
SSSSSSSSSSSS

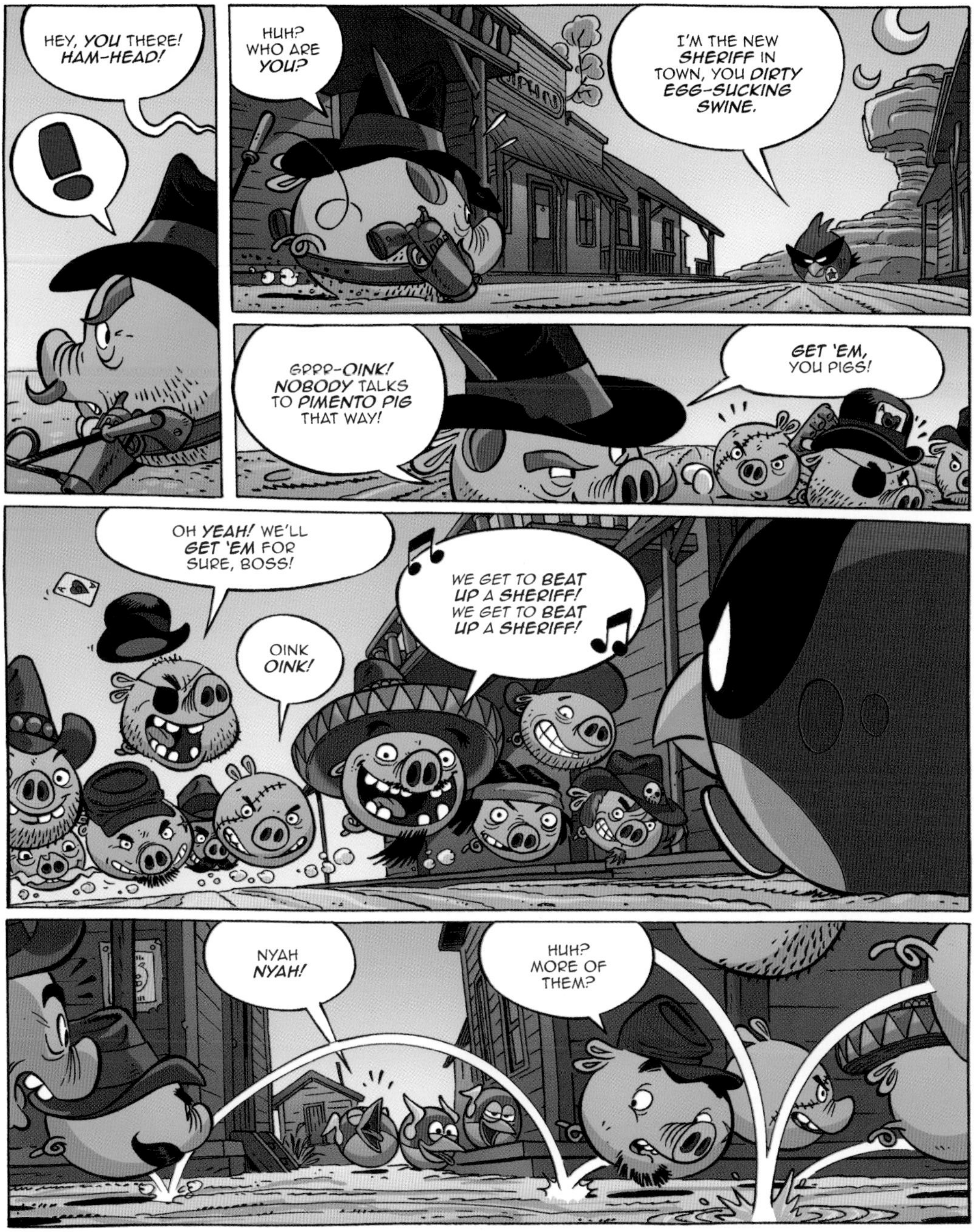
HEY, YOU THERE! HAM-HEAD!
!
HUH? WHO ARE YOU?
I'M THE NEW SHERIFF IN TOWN, YOU DIRTY EGG-SUCKING SWINE.
GRRR-OINK! NOBODY TALKS TO PIMENTO PIG THAT WAY!
GET 'EM, YOU PIGS!
OH YEAH! WE'LL GET 'EM FOR SURE, BOSS!
OINK OINK!
WE GET TO BEAT UP A SHERIFF! WE GET TO BEAT UP A SHERIFF!
NYAH NYAH!
HUH? MORE OF THEM?

AFTER THEM!
DON'T LET 'EM GET AWAY!
KAAA-WHAM!
YAYYYYYYY!
PANCAKES!

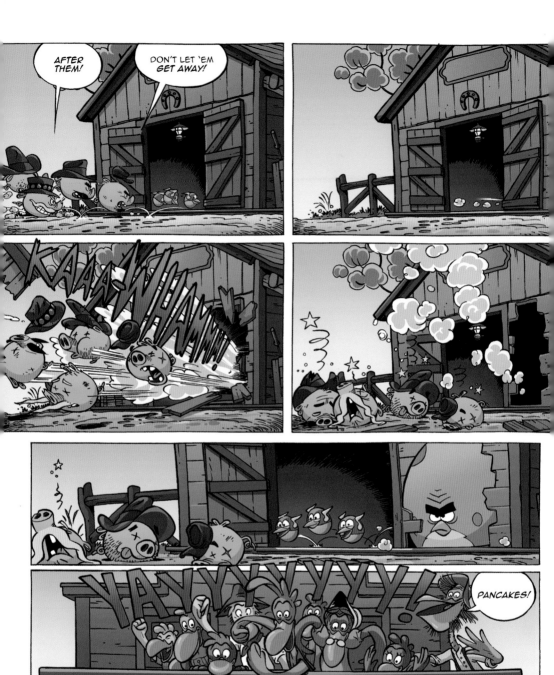

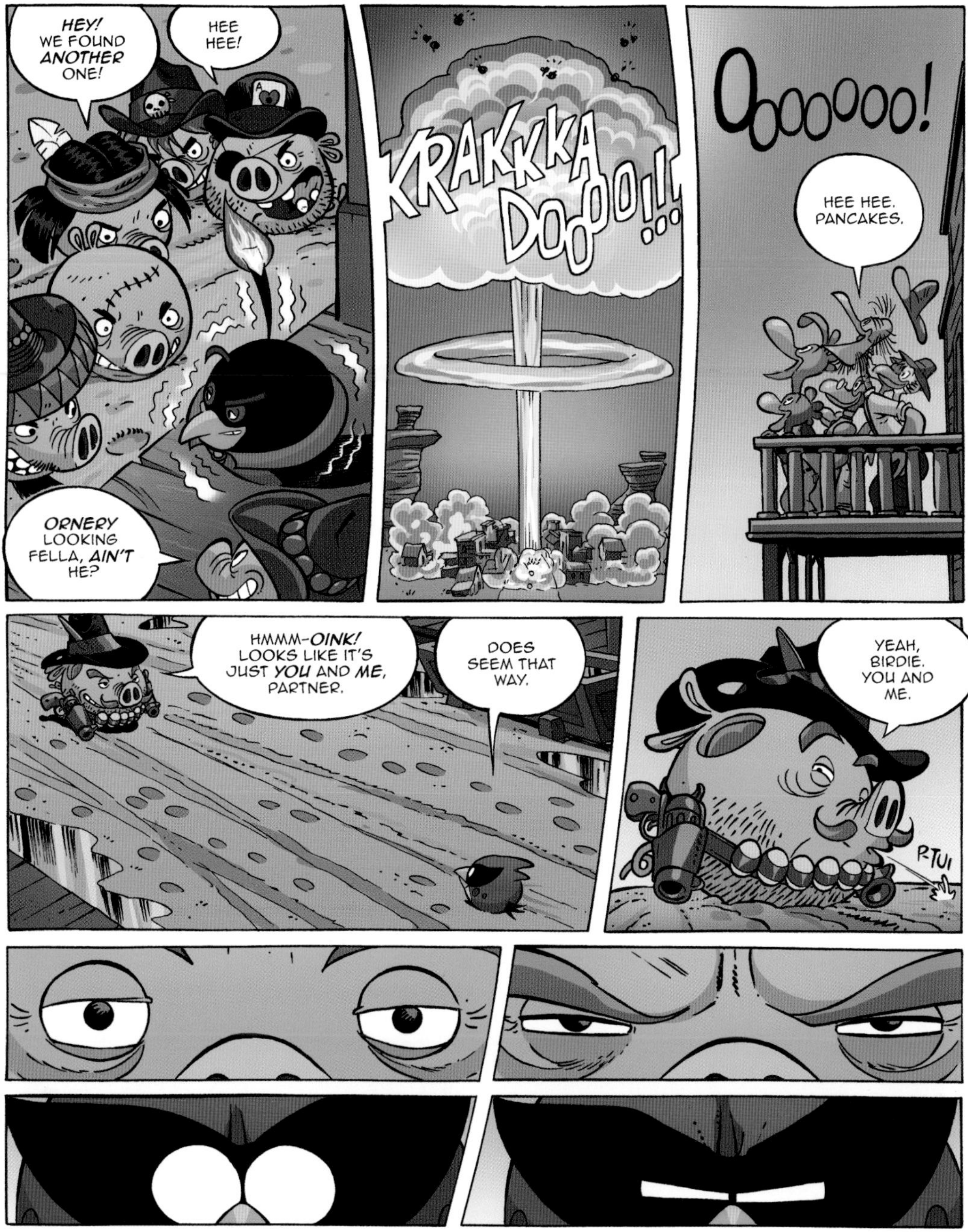
HEY! WE FOUND ANOTHER ONE!
HEE HEE!
ORNERY LOOKING FELLA, AIN'T HE?
KRAKKKA DOOOOO!!!
OOOOOOO!
HEE HEE. PANCAKES.
HMMM-OINK! LOOKS LIKE IT'S JUST YOU AND ME, PARTNER.
DOES SEEM THAT WAY.
YEAH, BIRDIE. YOU AND ME.
P-TUI

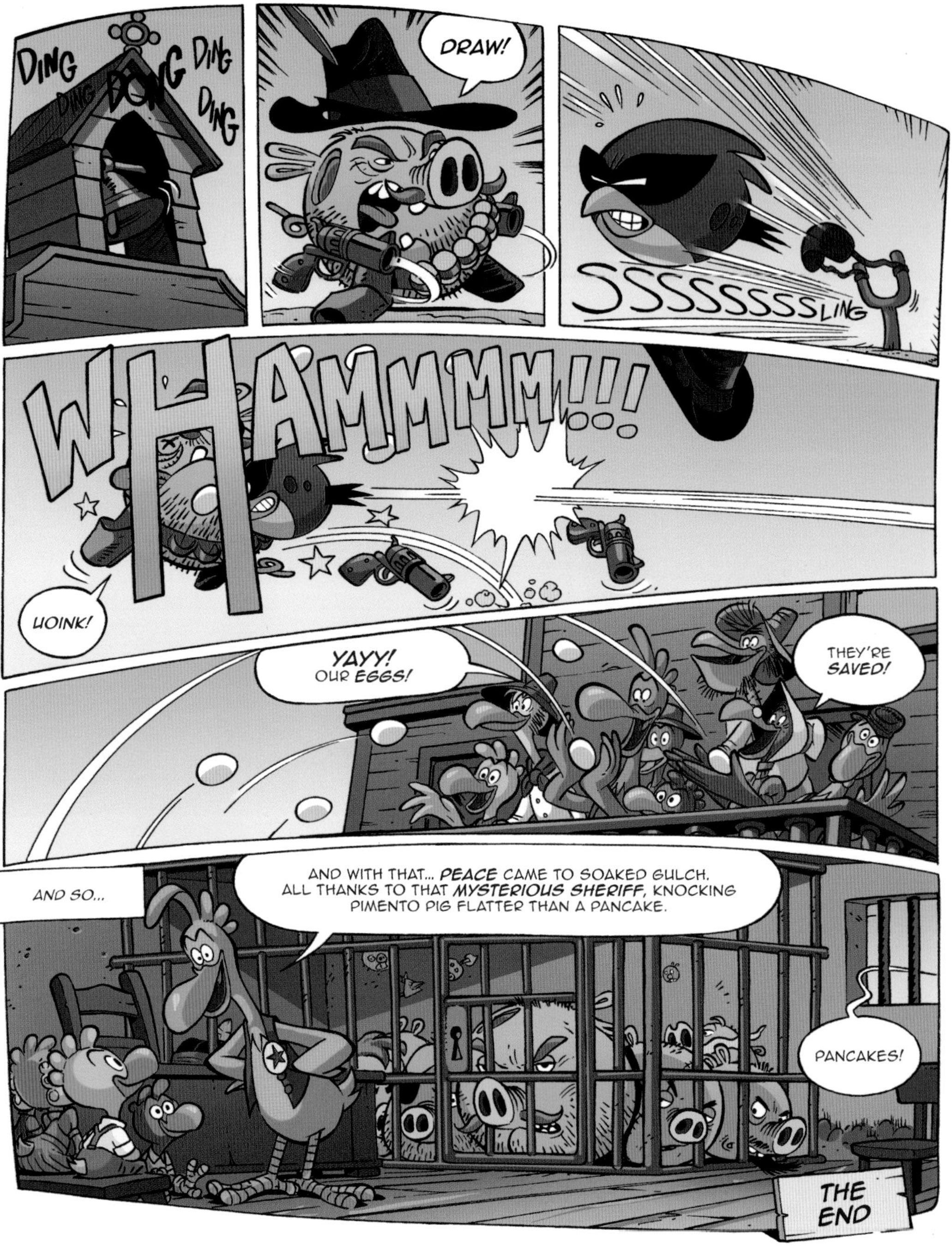
DING DING DONG DING DING
DRAW!
SSSSSSSSSLING
WHAMMMMM!!!
UOINK!
YAYY! OUR EGGS!
THEY'RE SAVED!
AND SO...
AND WITH THAT... PEACE CAME TO SOAKED GULCH. ALL THANKS TO THAT MYSTERIOUS SHERIFF, KNOCKING PIMENTO PIG FLATTER THAN A PANCAKE.
PANCAKES!
THE END

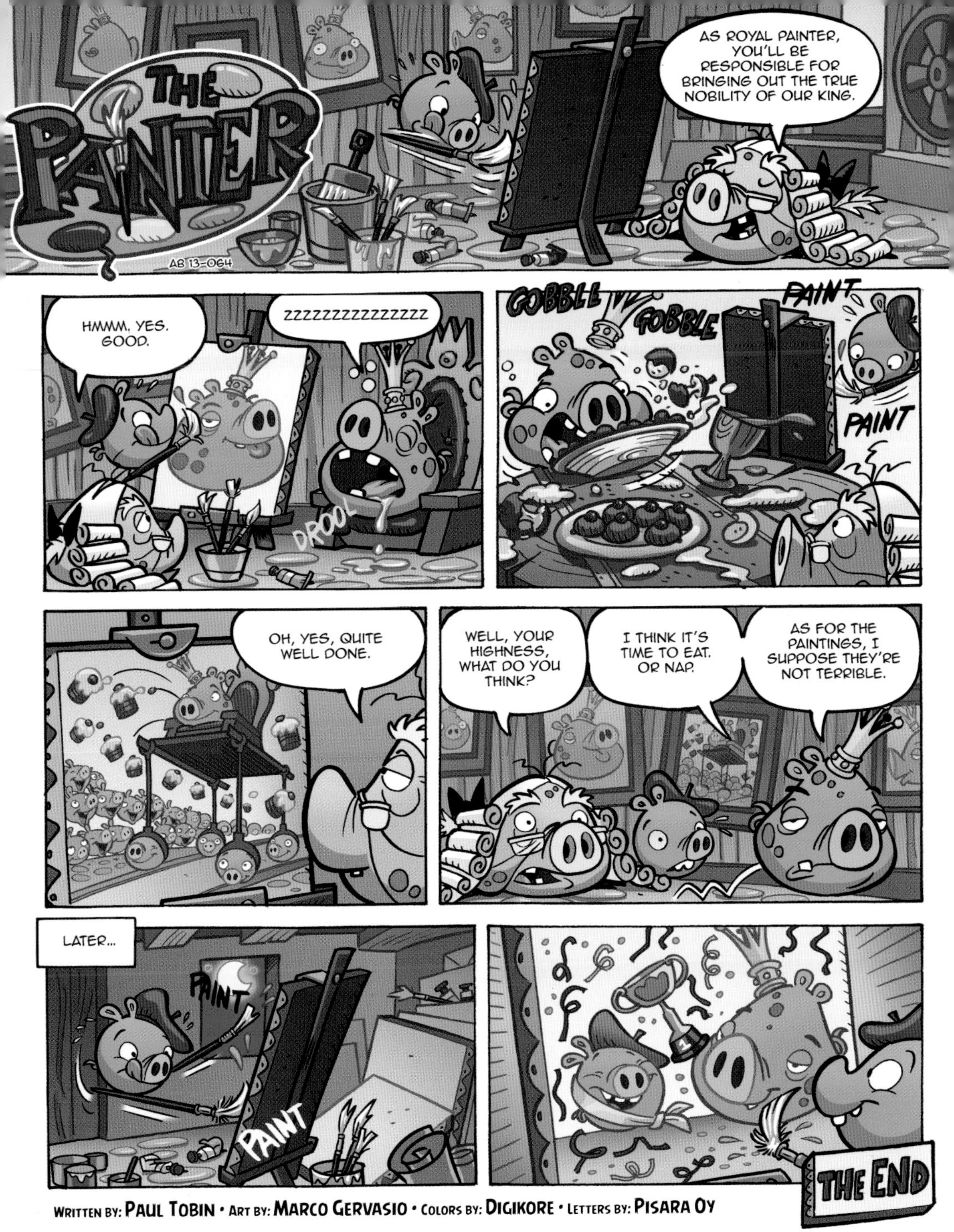
THE PAINTER
AB 13-064
AS ROYAL PAINTER, YOU'LL BE RESPONSIBLE FOR BRINGING OUT THE TRUE NOBILITY OF OUR KING.
HMMM. YES. GOOD.
ZZZZZZZZZZZZZZZ
DROOL
GOBBLE
GOBBLE
PAINT
PAINT
OH, YES, QUITE WELL DONE.
WELL, YOUR HIGHNESS, WHAT DO YOU THINK?
I THINK IT'S TIME TO EAT. OR NAP.
AS FOR THE PAINTINGS, I SUPPOSE THEY'RE NOT TERRIBLE.
LATER...
PAINT
PAINT
THE END

WRITTEN BY: PAUL TOBIN • ART BY: MARCO GERVASIO • COLORS BY: DIGIKORE • LETTERS BY: PISARA OY

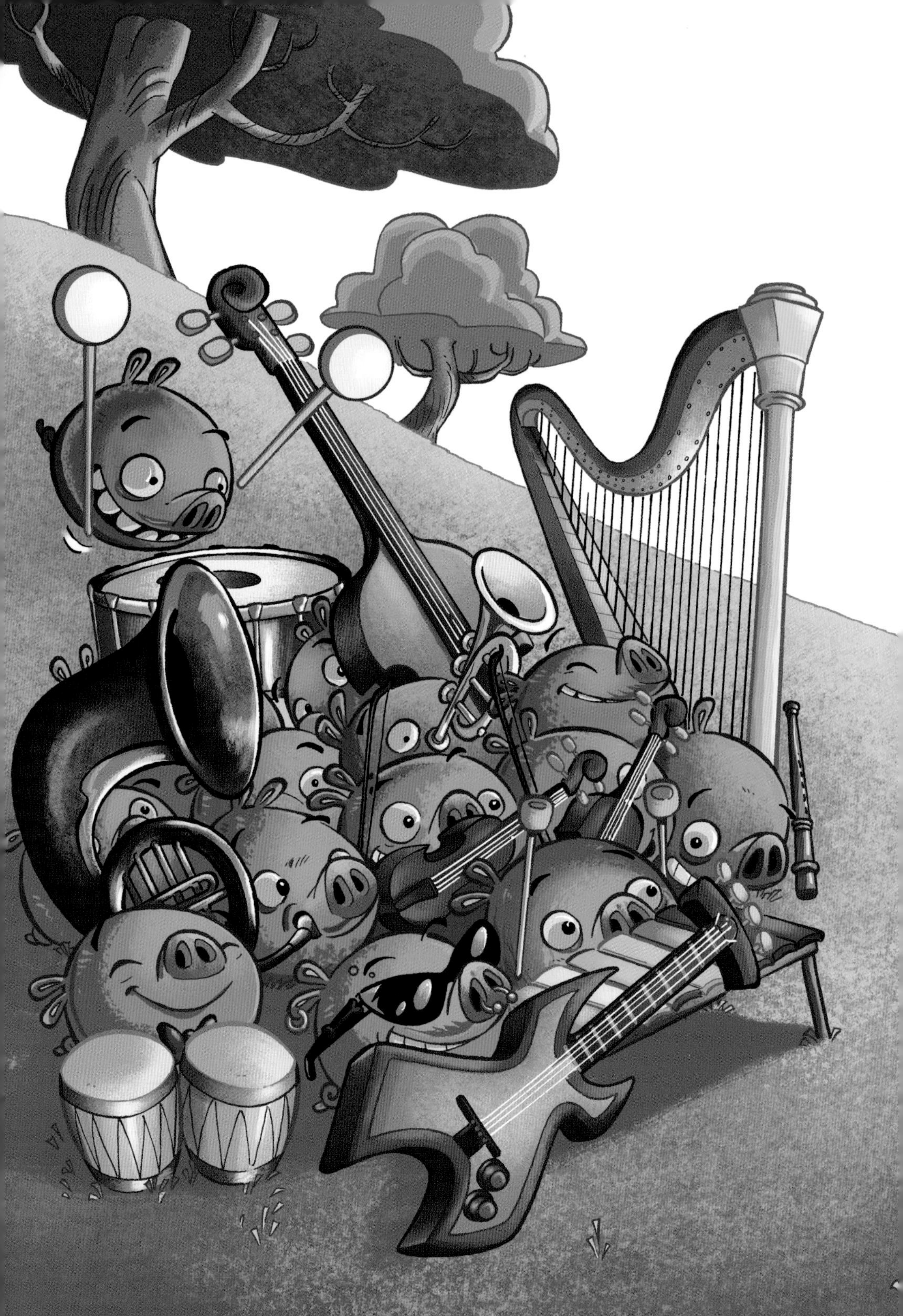

IDEA BY UPL
ARTWORK BY PACO RODRIQUES
COLORS BY DIGIKORE

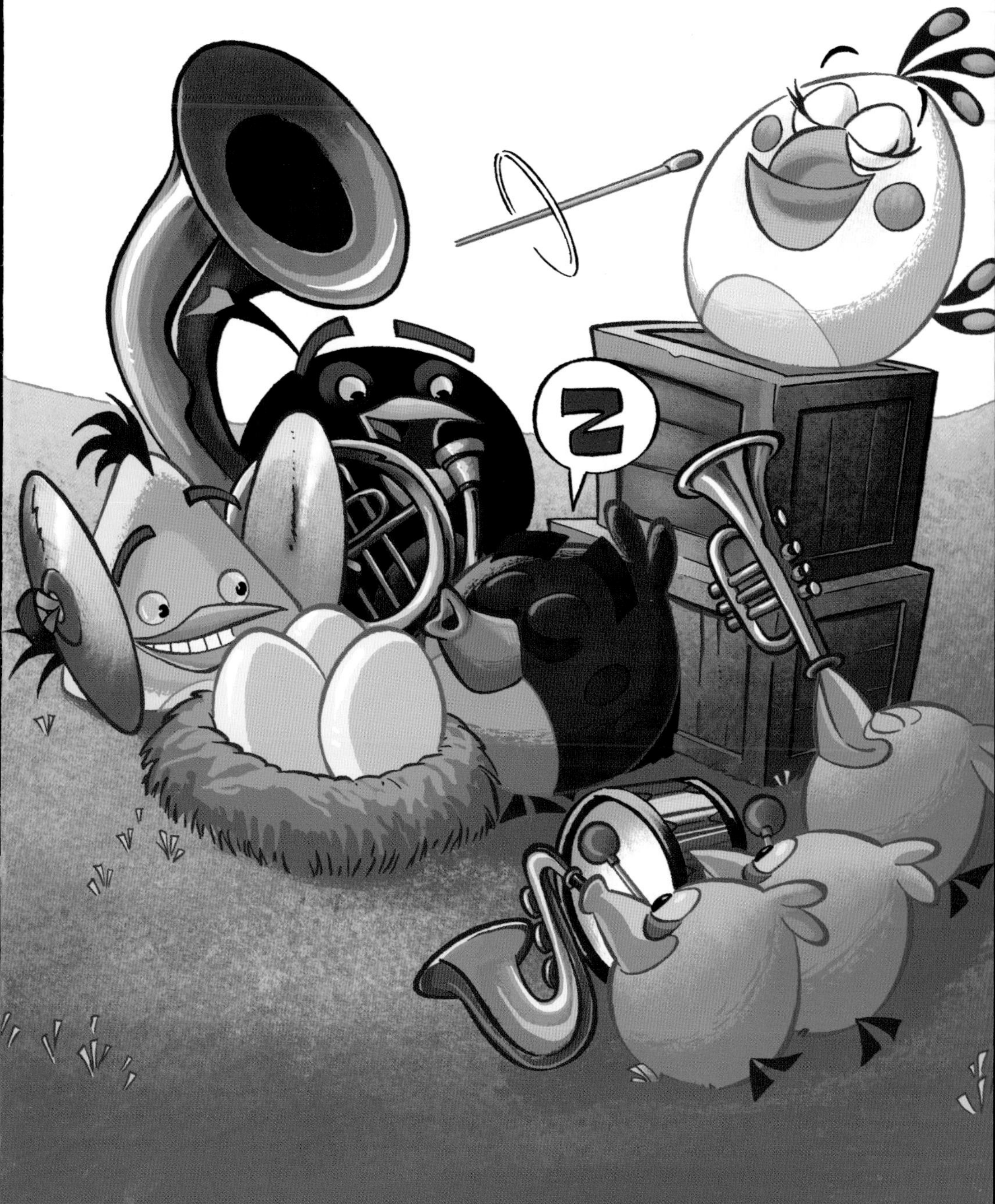
Z